For more than forty years,
Yearling has been the leading name
in classic and award-winning literature
for young readers.

Yearling books feature children's
favorite authors and characters,
providing dynamic stories of adventure,
humor, history, mystery, and fantasy.

Trust Yearling paperbacks to entertain,
inspire, and promote the love of reading
in all children.

OTHER YEARLING BOOKS YOU WILL ENJOY

SKELLIG, *David Almond*

INSIDE GRANDAD, *Peter Dickinson*

THE TEARS OF THE SALAMANDER, *Peter Dickinson*

THE QUILT, *Gary Paulsen*

GIFTS FROM THE SEA, *Natalie Kinsey-Warnock*

THE UNSEEN, *Zilpha Keatley Snyder*

THE LEGACY OF GLORIA RUSSELL, *Sheri Gilbert*

BLACKWATER BEN, *William Durbin*

GRASS ANGEL, *Julie Schumacher*

THE TRIAL, *Jennifer Bryant*

THE
FIRE-EATERS

DAVID
ALMOND

A YEARLING BOOK

Published by Yearling, an imprint of Random House Children's Books
a division of Random House, Inc., New York

Visit us on the Web! www.randomhouse.com/kids

Educators and librarians, for a variety of teaching tools, visit us at
www.randomhouse.com/teachers

ISBN: 0-440-42012-1

Reprinted by arrangement with Delacorte Press

Printed in the United States of America

November 2005

10 9 8 7 6 5 4 3 2

OPM

For Isabel Boissier

❄ ONE ❄

It all starts on the day I met McNulty. I was with my mam. We left Dad at home beside the sea. We took the bus to Newcastle. We got out below the statue of the angel, then headed down toward the market by the river. She was all in red. She kept singing "The Keel Row" and swinging my arm to the rhythm of the song. A crowd had gathered beyond the market stalls but we couldn't see what held so many people there. She led me closer. She stood on tiptoes. There were bodies all around me, blocking out the light. Seagulls were squealing. It had been raining. There were puddles in the joints between the cobblestones. I kicked water across my shiny new black shoes. The splashes turned to dark stains on my jeans. The water splashed on her ankles as well but she didn't seem to feel it. I tugged her hand and wanted to move away, but she didn't seem to feel it.

His voice was muffled by the bodies, and at first it

seemed so distant. "Pay!" he yelled. "You'll not see nowt till you pay!" I tugged her hand again. "Are you not listening?" he yelled. I raised my eyes and tried to see. And she put her hands beneath my arms and lifted me and I teetered on my toes and there he was, at the center of us all. I looked into his eyes. He looked back into mine. And it was as if my heart stopped beating and the world stopped turning. That was when it started. That moment, that Sunday, late summer, 1962.

He was a small, wild-eyed, bare-chested man. His skin was covered in scars and bruises. There were rough and faded tattoos of beasts and women and dragons. He had a little canvas sack on a long stick. He kept shoving it at the crowd.

"Pay!" he yelled and snarled. "You'll not get nowt till you pay."

Some of the crowd turned away and pushed past us as we moved forward. They shook their heads and rolled their eyes. He was pathetic, they said. He was a fake. One of them leaned close to Mam. "Take the lad away," he said. "Some of the tricks is just disgusting. Not for bairns to see. It shouldn't be allowed."

McNulty's hair was black. He had pointed gold teeth at the front of his mouth and he wore tiny golden earrings. There were deep creases in his cheeks. The bridge was high behind him. The sun shone through its arch. Steam and scents from the hot dog stalls and popcorn makers drifted across us. Mam held me against her.

"Reach into my pocket," she said. "Find him a coin."

I reached down and took out some silver. When I looked up again his little sack was right before my eyes.

"Into the sack with it, bonny lad," he said.

I dropped the coin in. He held my eye with his. He grinned.

"Good lad," he snarled.

He took the sack away.

"Pay," he yelled, shoving the sack at other faces. "Get your money out and pay!"

She pushed my shoulders, helping me forward. I squirmed through, right to the front of the crowd.

"Bonny lad!" he muttered when he saw me there. He looked through the crowd. "Bonny lady."

The stick and the sack were on the ground. He flexed his muscles. A cart wheel lay on the cobbles beside him. He stood it on end, in front of him. It had heavy wooden spokes, a thick steel rim. It was as high as his chest.

"Could McNulty lift this?" he hissed.

He took it in his hands, spread his legs, bent his knees and lifted it to his thighs and let it rest there.

"Could he?" he said through gritted teeth. "Could he?"

There were tears of strain in his eyes.

He groaned, lifted again, a sudden jerk that took the cart wheel high. We gasped. We backed away. He leaned his head back and rested the wheel on his brow so that it stood above him, with the sun and the bridge caught in its ring. He shuffled on the cobbles, balancing himself with his elbows wide and his hands gripping the rim of steel. He grunted and hissed. Then he lifted the cart wheel free and let it fall with a crash and the whole earth seemed to shake.

He glared at us. He blinked, wiped his tears away.

"See? See what a man can do?"

I reached behind me but Mam's hand wasn't there. I looked back through the crowd and saw her and she smiled and held up her hand, telling me to stay there.

"What next?" said McNulty. "The fire or the chains or the . . ."

He fell silent as his eye met mine again. He leaned close.

"Help me, bonny," he whispered.

He reached for my hand. I turned to Mam. She waved again and smiled, as if to tell me everything was fine, she was still there, there was nothing to fear. He cupped my shoulder and drew me to him. Dozens of eyes watched.

"This is my assistant," he said. "His name is . . ."

I couldn't speak. He leaned close. He cupped his hand across his mouth, whispered into my ear.

"His name is . . ."

"R-Robert," I stammered.

"R-Robert!" he announced.

He crouched in front of me. His skin glistened. I caught the smoky sweaty scent of him. I caught the sour smell of the river flowing darkly nearby. I looked into the black center of his eyes.

"There is a box here, bonny," he told me.

He slid a casket to my feet.

"Open it," he said.

I did nothing.

"Open it, Bobby," he whispered.

With trembling fingers, I opened it. Inside were needles and pins and fishhooks and skewers and knives and scissors, some of them all rusted, some of them all bright.

"Take out something awful," he said. "Take out the thing that you think should make the most pain."

I stared into his eyes, so deep and dark.

"Do it, Bobby," he said.

I took out a silver skewer, as long as my forearm. It had a Saracen's head as a handle. The point was needle-sharp.

He shuddered.

"Well chosen, Bobby."

He stood up. He held the skewer between his index fingers for the crowd to see.

"Who would dare?" he said. "Bobby!"

I looked up at him.

"Bobby, pass the sack to them. Tell them to put their coins in it. Tell them they'll not see nowt until they pay."

I just wanted to escape, but the bodies were packed before me. The faces were all smiles. Mam had her hand across her mouth. She widened her eyes, she raised her shoulders, she tried to go on smiling.

"Do it, Bobby," he said. "Do the buggers think a man like me can live on fresh air? Pay! Tell them! Get your money out and pay!"

I weakly pushed the sack into the crowd. McNulty barked his demands. Mam leaned far toward me, dropped three coins in. I wanted to reach out to her, grab her hand, get her to pull me away. Then McNulty snapped:

"Enough, Bobby. They're tightfisted crooks and they won't give us what we need. But to hell with them. Let's give them something to infect their waking and fire their dreams."

I turned to him. He touched my cheek. He drew me to his side. He spoke to me as if no one else existed, as if there were just the two of us there beside the river on that brightening late-summer day.

"Help me, son," he said.

He stood stock-still. He lowered his head, closed his eyes. He breathed deeply. He muttered incomprehensible words. He raised his head, opened his eyes. He held the point of the skewer against his cheek. He looked blankly at the crowd.

"Bobby," he said. "Touch me if I cry out. Catch me if I fall."

My heart began to race. I could hardly catch my breath. He held the Saracen's head and pushed. The point of the skewer entered his cheek. He blinked and sighed. He pushed again. The skewer slid further in. A tiny trickle of blood fell down his cheek. He smiled, at nothing, at no one. Many in the crowd recoiled in fear and disgust. The skewer slid further. Soon it pressed against the inside of his other cheek. He kept pushing and the point broke through and another tiny trickle of blood fell from his other cheek. Now he held the skewer still, one fingertip resting on the Saracen's head, another on the needle point. He grinned out at the crowd. He opened his mouth, slowly turned his head from side to side and everyone leaned close, to see the metal stretched between his teeth, across his throat. There were giggles and groans, yelps of disgust.

He crouched before me again, as if to show me, just me.

Then he pulled the Saracen's head, and slowly drew the skewer out. He licked his lips, brushed his bloody cheeks with the back of his hand. He wiped the skewer on his forearm and passed it to me.

"Back in its box, Bobby," he said.

I put it back into its box. I closed the lid. I shuddered. I could hardly breathe. I started to shuffle away.

"Don't leave me, Bobby," he said.

I shook my head, backed away. I twisted my head. Mam reached out to me, beckoned me to her.

"At least don't go without your pay," he said.

He drew me back to him.

"Thank you," he said.

He pressed a silver coin onto my palm.

"We'll mebbes meet again," he said, and a tiny splash of blood fell from his lips across our joined hands.

Then he let me go, and the crowd parted, and let me get through to my mam, while behind me McNulty already snarled and snapped again.

"What's next? The fire? No, we're not ready for the fire and the madness of the fire! The chains? Get your money out and pay! You'll not see nowt till you pay!"

❧ TWO ❧

We twisted and turned through the crowds between the stalls. Mam picked up trinkets and scarves and dropped them back again.

"It's all rubbish," she whispered. "Rubbish and tat."

She took out a white shirt from its cellophane and held it against me. She smiled with delight.

"You'll look so grand," she said.

She tugged at the seams, she held the shirt up to the sun, she twisted her face and pondered, then passed a couple of pounds over.

She laughed.

"It'll shrink. I know it. But you'll look great. You'll be the proper little man."

We ate hot beef sandwiches, smeared them with sauce and mustard, licked the juices that ran down our chins and across our fingers. We drank bittersweet sarsaparilla from a health stall. Then we moved away from the stalls and walked right by the water's edge. It flowed ten feet below us. Seagulls hovered over the water and swooped for the scraps thrown by a bunch of children. The tide was turning and the center was all eddies and swirls and agitation. Mam kept laughing, holding her face up to the sun.

"I told your dad the day would brighten," she said. "He's an old misery! All that autumn and winter nonsense!"

And she took my hand and hurried me forward.

"Come on!" she said. "Let's ride a lift up to the sky!"

The lift was inside the stone column of the bridge. We stood in the shade of the bridge's great steel arch. I spread my hands across its huge rivets. Traffic roared high above us. Nearby, a herring gull ripped at something bloody in a brown paper sack. A river bell rang, a distant ship hooted.

When the lift came down, there was a little man inside sitting on a stool.

"Come in, madam," he called. "And you, young sir!"

He pressed his buttons and pulled his levers. I saw how he couldn't keep his eyes off her as we shuddered up toward the sky. On a shelf at his side were a Thermos flask, a sandwich box, and a notebook and a pen. He saw me looking.

"I keep a note of everyone," he said. His eyes sparkled. "All my customers. Just for memory's sake."

I wanted to reach out, lift the book, look inside, and he knew it.

"Ah, to you it would be simply boring," he said. "It's nothing but dates and descriptions and weather reports." He shrugged. "I must do something to fill my days of rise and fall, rise and fall, rise and fall."

He took the coin she handed him and opened the door with a flourish.

"Here we are, then. Farewell, madam. Farewell, young sir!"

We stepped out onto the platform of the bridge. As the doors closed, he was already writing.

"Beautiful bright lady," I heard him say. "All dressed in red. Her quiet boy. September 2nd, 1962. Sunshine after rain."

The lift door closed. Buses and trucks and cars trundled past us. There was a stink of exhaust smoke. Mam stood at the parapet and stared down toward the river and the market. I crouched beside her and looked through the metal palings. The river swirled. Seagulls flew below us. Down at the market's edge, we saw the crowd around McNulty. He was wrapped in chains. He writhed and jerked and struggled on the cobbles.

"Look at him," she said. "The poor soul."

She tipped her head forward so that her hair fell down in front of me. She leaned further and her upside-down face came into view. She smiled at me from the dizzying space outside the bridge. Then she laughed and started running. The red coat opened and rose around her like wings.

"Come on, Bobby!" she called. "Run! Race you to the other side!"

❧ THREE ❧

We walked back into the city. We waited for the bus beside the war memorial. The angel with her sword looked down on us. Struggling ranks of stone soldiers reached up to her. Someone had painted BAN THE BOMB in white across the densely packed names of the city's dead. In the bus I let Mam put her arm around me and we leaned together as we rattled past the city's edge. I tried to listen to her heart. She said the sky was beautiful, the way its blueness faded into countless shades of purple and orange and pink. She praised the fields, the hedgerows, the allotments, the pigeon lofts, the silhouettes of pitheads to the north. She gasped at the first sight of the distant glistening sea, at the rooftops of our Keely Bay.

"It's like...," she said. "But who could catch such beauty?"

"You," I murmured, much too softly for her to hear.

"You," she said. "You're such a quiet one these days. What happened to our little laughing wild lad?" She squeezed my hand. "Not to worry. It's a stage. The laughing lad'll soon come back again. Oh, just look at Mister Organizer!"

There was Dad, waiting at the junction by the Rat, with his arm held high to stop the bus. She stamped her foot when she jumped down.

"Do you think we're too daft to get off at the right stop?" she said.

Then she giggled and kissed him.

"What a time we've had!" she said. "Markets and bridges and strongmen. Tell him, Bobby. Tell him what you did! Come on!"

We set off arm in arm along the lane toward the sea. We passed the post office, its window packed with fishing nets, comics, tin cars and soldiers, fake dog turds, buckets and spades. I gathered my thoughts.

"There was this man called McNulty...," I started, but she butted in straightaway.

"Man?" She laughed. "Man? He was a devil, a demon, a rascal...and guess who he picked out from the crowd!"

We all laughed as she told the tale of the wild man with his skewers and chains, and of little quivering me, his helper. Then Dad was silent for a while.

"Small, black-haired, tattoos?" he said. "McNulty?"

"Yes," I told him.

"I knew him."

"You knew him?" I said.

"Aye." He shook his head and stared into the empty sky. "But I thought he'd be surely dead by now."

Mam looked at him, wide-eyed.

"Howay, then, mister," she said. "Tell us the tale."

He laughed softly. The lane opened out to the scruffy edge of the beach. There was a rutted turning circle for cars and carts. We walked through to the beach, where fragments of sharp coal mingled with the soft beige sand.

"*Come on,*" said Mam.

"It was the end of the war," he said. "All them years back. Nineteen forty-five, the year they let us come home. He was on the same boat as me, coming back from Burma. He was one of them that'd seen too much, suffered too much. It was like his brain'd been boiled. Too much war, too much heat, too many magic men. The man was such a mess. Little McNulty, eh? Fancy him lasting all this time."

It was darkening. Stars came out. The lighthouse light began to turn. We walked toward the sea.

"He was the ship's fool. Mostly we put up with him, or laughed at him. His mind was all gone. Chants and spells and curses and dances. Them things he did with ropes and swords and fire. There was them that said he was a proper magic man. There was some that humored him or tried to care for him. It was clear he was going to

need looking after. But some of the blokes . . . There's no
end to cruelty, is there? One morning I found him in a
heap on the stairs with his clothes all ripped and his
skull cracked and blood all over him. What's happened?
I says to him. Nowt, he says. Nowt. But he's crying like
a bairn. He flinches. When I touch him his eyes is like a
little desperate dog's. And the whimpering he made . . . I
found a nurse and he never flinched while she stitched
him. He just stroked my arm and said I was a bonny
bonny lad. Poor soul."

"Wonder what brings him here now," said Mam.

"God knows," said Dad.

The lighthouse light turned. It became more bril-
liant as the daylight faded. We stood and breathed the
sea air. We watched a late tern diving at the sea. Further
along the beach, the sea coalers and their ponies
dragged carts filled with coal from the sea. There was a
girl's laughter and I peered toward it through the dusk.
The air calmed. The sea calmed. It stretched like bur-
nished metal to the dark dead-flat horizon. The lighthouse light became a beam that swept the sea, the land
and then the sea again. We were silent and still. We
hardly breathed, as if we didn't dare disturb such peace.
Then Mam sighed at last. Dad lit a cigarette and drew
deeply on it.

"Such a world we live in," said Mam.

She smiled. She nudged Dad.

"So, Mister Chef," she said. "What wonders have you prepared to welcome us home?"

"A banquet," he said. "Come and see."

We headed to our house above the beach. A light burned in the window. Pale smoke rose from the chimney.

"McNulty," said Dad. "You'll have to take me, Bobby, show me where he was. Mebbe he'll be back in the same place again. Who'd believe it, after all these years." He opened the little gate into our garden. He squeezed my arm. "He was always harmless, son. Don't be hexed by him."

❧ FOUR ❧

We had his little pasties hot from the oven, with carrots and potatoes whipped into a cream. He gave me half a glassful of his beer. There was rice pudding, sweet and rich beneath its scorched skin. We mixed jam into it and sighed at such deliciousness. The lights were low, the curtains open. Every minute the window filled with light. Dad's thoughts kept turning to the war, to his voyage home, to McNulty.

"Skin!" he said. "He said loads of stuff about skin. He said he'd seen men who dressed in the skin of a beast and became the beast. Men in lion skins snarling like lions. Men in antelope skins leaping like antelopes. Tiger skin, ape skin, snake skin. Put them on, he said, say the proper words, and you can turn to anything."

I rubbed my hand. A mark was left where McNulty's tiny drops of blood had fallen. Or was it a mark I'd always had? I fingered the coin he'd given me in payment. I recalled his breath, his skin, his deep dark driven eyes.

Dad lit a cigarette. His breath rasped as he inhaled. I cleared the table with Mam. In the kitchen, she crossed off yet another day from the calendar.

"Just another week till that new school," she said, and she beamed at me.

The air grew cold. Dad threw more sea coal and lumps of driftwood onto the fire. I sat with him and watched TV. There'd been more nuclear bomb tests in Russia and the USA. President Kennedy stood at a lectern, whispered to a general, shuffled some papers and spoke of his resolution, our growing strength. He said there were no limits to the steps we'd take if we were pushed. Khrushchev made a fist, thumped a table and glared. Then came the pictures that accompanied such reports: the missiles that would be launched, the planes that would take off, the mushroom clouds, the howling winds, the devastated cities.

Dad spat into the fire. He cursed and lit another cigarette.

"This isn't enough for them," he said. "This quiet, this beauty, this peace. Listen to them. They're animals, howling for blood."

He inhaled.

"Maybe we should go far away," he said. "Where none of their nonsense can ever reach us."

"Australia!" called Mam.

She came through the door with my school uniform in her hands.

"Australia! That's what it was going to be. I'll take you away to where it's hot and clean and new. That's what he said. Australia, my love! A new life! Come on. Put this on, bonny boy. Let me make those changes."

She drew me to her, put the blazer on me and giggled. She knelt beside me with pins gripped in her teeth. She snapped down my sleeves, turned up the cuffs to the level of my wrists, and tacked them with pins.

"Keep straight," she kept saying. "You'll finish no quicker by jiggling about.

"Anybody'd think you'd be proud," she said.

I sighed and rolled my eyes at Dad and watched the window and let her have her way. The heat of the fire scorched my legs.

"There," she said. "Now let me look at you."

She pushed me away and sat back on her heels.

"Fasten it up properly, then. That's right."

I saw the tears in their eyes as they smiled at each other.

"Bobby," she said. "Put it all on. Go on, love, with the new shirt. Go on. It won't take long."

I stood there.

"Go on, eh?" said Dad.

In my room I stripped off my jeans and sweater and put on everything: the socks and flannel shorts, the white shirt, the dark tie. I tied on the heavy black shiny shoes. And I replaced the blazer, the too-long, too-wide covering of black with golden battlements shining from its pocket.

"Oh, Bobby," she whispered when I went back down. "Oh, Bobby. What a man."

Then there came a knocking at the door. A deep voice called in from the dark.

"Bobby! You in, Bobby? You coming out?"

Mam's face darkened.

"Joseph Connor," she said.

She looked at her watch.

"It's too late," she said.

"Bobby!" Joseph called.

"He's too old," said Mam.

She looked at Dad, and he smiled.

"Come on, love," he said. "It's still holiday. Give him half an hour, eh?"

She clicked her tongue.

"Not a moment more."

❧ FIVE ❧

I yelled that I'd be just a minute. I went upstairs and changed again. I ran into the dark. He was nowhere to be seen. I crossed the lane toward the beach. When the lighthouse light came round I saw a body draped across a heap of seaweed. It rose and leapt at me and wrestled me to the sand.

"That was a pretty uniform I seen you in," he whispered. "What a lovely little schoolboy you're gonna make!"

I twisted and kneed him in the crotch. I rolled him over and sat on him and pressed his shoulders to the earth.

"A pity that some of us is just too bloody thick to make the grade," I said.

He roared and shoved me off. I ran full pelt from him toward the sea.

"Come and catch me, Dumbo!" I yelled.

"I'll get you, nancy boy!" he answered.

We ran a quarter mile or so. I waited for him at the water's edge. We leaned forward, grasped our knees, gasped for breath, roared with laughter. The water soaked the sand around our feet. He put his arm around me.

"What'll we do?" I said.

He took ten Players from his pocket. I shook my head when he offered me one. He lit up and breathed out a plume of smoke. I turned my face away. I saw flashing airplane lights move across the stars.

"Let's go down the new kid's way," he said.

We walked on. We were bathed in light, then plunged into the dark.

"I saw an escapologist today," I said.

"Aye? I seen Ailsa. She was asking where you were."

"I saw him stick a skewer right through his cheeks."

"I seen her again with her dad in the water getting coal. Not a stitch on her legs, Bobby."

"He had this . . . dunno. Power in him."

"Should've seen her. She says she's not gonna go to your school, you know."

"I know. She's daft."

"She says she doesn't see why she should just 'cos she's proved she can."

"So she'll go to your place?"

"Doubt she'll go anywhere. You know what they're like, that lot."

"Aye." I shook my head. "She's daft."

The new kid's house was where another of the lanes

came down onto the beach. It had been a fisherman's place; then it had become derelict and half buried in the sand. Now there were a garage and some new rooms at the back and a huge window at the front facing out across the sea.

We shut up as we got closer. We walked with our heads lowered and our knees bent. We crouched at the dried-out battered knee-high fence. The curtains were open. The new kid was sitting on a box, reading a magazine, holding his hair back with his hand. There were boxes all around him. His dad was stretched out on a sofa with a book. His mam took a record out from its cover, put it on a record player. The sound of drums and saxophones drifted into the night.

"Bloody jazz," said Joseph.

We watched. We kept ducking when the light came round. The new kid's dad poured some wine. The new kid swayed, like he was half dancing. Somebody said something and they all laughed together.

"Seen them by the lighthouse, on the headland," said Joseph. "They had sandwiches and that. They were taking photos."

"He's called Daniel," I said.

"Aye. He's a jessie, eh? Look at him."

He lit another cigarette.

"Don't," I said. "They'll see."

"No, they won't. Light inside, dark outside, they'll never see nowt."

He breathed out smoke.

"He'll be with you," he said. "He'll be at your school. Him and you and all the other nancy boys."

"Don't be stupid."

"What?"

"Nowt."

"Huh. Look at them."

He threw his cigarette away and stood up and climbed across the fence. He crouched low and prowled toward the window.

"Joseph, man!" I whispered.

He stood up right in front of the window. He spread his arms wide like he was daring them to see him. He stuck two fingers up at the window with both hands.

"Joseph!" I whispered. "Joseph!"

The light came round and swept across his back. The new kid jumped from his box. His dad sat up. Joseph turned and ran and vaulted the fence and raced into the darkness of the beach. I followed close behind. After a couple of hundred yards he went sprawling. He giggled and grunted as I threw myself down beside him. He cursed the new kid and his family. I laughed; then I sighed and said I'd have to go.

"You're stupid," I said.

He got me by the throat. He shoved my face into the sand.

"Don't call me stupid," he snarled. "Bloody never. Right?"

I tried to speak but couldn't.

"Right?" he said.

I twisted my head. I tried to spit, dribbled sand and saliva.

"Right," I muttered.

He gave me one last shove, one last curse; then he got up and went away.

✾ SIX ✾

I watched Joseph disappear; then I took my shoes and socks off and waded into the icy sea. I scooped up water and rinsed my mouth. I thought I tasted blood but it might have just been the salt. The night was clear and bright. I tried to discern the horizon, to see where the stars became the reflections of stars. I watched the airplane lights. I tried to distinguish the far-off roar of engines from the ever-present rumble of the sea. I looked toward the east. If the bombers came, is that where they would come from? I tried to imagine them, great cross-shaped shadows, no lights, unmistakable roars. I tried to imagine everything destroyed: no beach, no dunes, no house, no family, no friends, no me. Nothing. Nothing left but poison sluggish sea and poison drifting dust.

I watched the massive cone of light approach me.

"Bobby!"

The call came from behind me.

"Bobby, is it you?"

I turned. Ailsa. The light swept over her, and her eyes glittered and her face bloomed.

She laughed and came in beside me.

"I was looking for you today," she said.

"I know."

"Daddy said you could have come and helped us. He would have paid you, Bobby."

"Mebbe another time."

"He says he can always use another hand."

We stood knee-deep in the water. I could feel the tiny fragments of coal swirling around my skin.

"Daddy says it's the sailors," she said.

"What is?"

"That wailing. Can you hear it?"

I listened. Was it something, or was it just imagination?

"Can you?" she said.

"What do you mean, sailors?"

"Dunno. A ship was torpedoed, and all hands were lost. In the last war, or another one. Not sure, really." We listened together. She laughed. "Or mebbe it's just another story Daddy made up and it's just the seals. But..."

And there they were, the sounds that could be howls and cries if we heard them in a certain way.

"Sometimes I've heard laughter," she said. "But nothing like this. What they howling for, Bobby?"

"It's just the air. It's just the sea. It's just..."

She touched my arm.

"You know it's not. Are you worried, too, Bobby Burns?"

"No. No."

"That's good."

"It's just that..." I felt my face coloring and I was glad of darkness. "...that it's all so..."

Then my name was called again.

"Bobby! Bobbeeeeee!"

"Beautiful," I said.

She laughed.

"Yes," she said. "I know."

"Boooobbeeeeeee!"

"I've got to go," I said.

She leaned to me and quickly kissed my cheek, and giggled, and pushed me on my way.

❄ SEVEN ❄

The fire roared. We kept the television and the radio off. Mam hummed "O Sacred Heart" as she stitched my blazer sleeves. Dad lifted a blazing coal from the fire with tongs to light his cigarette. The flames flickered before his lips. He drew smoke deeply in, gasped it out again, coughed, caught his breath, laughed at himself.

"Them damn things," said Mam. "When you going to pack them in?"

Dad winked at me.

"When tomorrow comes," he said, and he changed the subject to McNulty. "Mebbe he's there every Sunday morning," he said. "I should try to get to talk to him, eh?"

"Aye," I said.

"We'll go next Sunday. We'll take lots of coins for him."

We ate hot buttered toast and we smiled. I drifted. I

heard the turning of the sea. I must have fallen asleep. I saw the skewer and the blood. I heard his voice: Pay! You'll not get nothing till you pay!

Mam touched me.

"You're snoring," she said. "Just like you used to, years ago. Go on. Upstairs."

I heard them laughing fondly as I climbed.

I sat at the table before my window. I switched my Lourdes light on: the little plastic grotto with St. Bernadette on her knees and Mary smiling gently down. Mam had brought it back for me from the parish trip last year. "A present from a place of miracles," she'd said.

I found a notebook and I wrote.

Small, muscled, bare-chested man. McNulty. Joseph. The new kid. Ailsa. Drowned sailors, wailing. September 2nd, 1962. Sunshine after rain, then darkness. Autumn's on its way. What am I so scared of?

Then I lay in bed and dreamed again and the blankets became chains and my sleep was a great writhing and struggling to break free.

❧ EIGHT ❧

I was with Joseph. We were in the dunes beyond the headland. He stretched out with his hands behind his head. He had ice-blue jeans on and a black shirt and black pointed boots. I lay close by him and kept measuring myself against him. How would I ever get to be so big?

He was talking about the future, about what he'd be.

"It's still gonna be the building trade, like me dad," he said. "He says he'll easy get me a start. There's gonna be all kind of building going on in town. Offices and restaurants and hotels and the motorway. The work'll last for years. I cannot wait, man. Money in me pocket, pints of beer, lasses. Hey, look." He pulled his shirt up, turned over and showed me his back. "He had a good week last week, give us another quid, so I got the head filled in."

It was his tattoo, his dragon. The jaws with the massive teeth and the forked tongue gaped between his shoulders, the body with its scales and horns twisted all down his back, the legs with their great claws stretched around his sides, and the tail dipped down below his jeans. Most of it was outline, but bit by bit, when he could afford it, he was getting it filled in. When he'd talked about it first, I told him, Don't do it. You're too young, man. Think of when you're older. But he just laughed and cursed and called me a nance and said he was three years older than me anyway, so what did I know? In the end I even went with him to Blyth and I told the tattooist: Yes, of course he's sixteen.

"It's lovely," I said, and we grinned.

"Aye," he said. "It's lovely but you cannot stand it."

There was still some summer heat in the sun. There were a few families on the beach, sitting on blankets. Kids screamed and played in the shallows. Dogs plunged into the waves. The wooden beach café was open; its tattered flag was flying in the breeze. Somewhere an ice cream van played "Oh, Dear, What Can the Matter Be."

"But you," said Joseph. "You'll be something really fancy. And you'll clear off. And we'll never meet again."

"No, I won't."

"Yes, you will." He punched me and we giggled. "We

both know it. But never mind. Who could blame you? And we're still mates for now." And then he pointed. "Well, I never."

It was Daniel, all alone. He had his jeans turned up, and he was wading through the sea.

"What brings buggers like that to a place like this?" said Joseph.

"Me mam says they work in Newcastle."

"Aye, but why come here? Keely Bay! It's nowt but coaly beaches and coaly sea and nowt going on. It's bliddy derelict, man. It's had its day."

I looked around: the dunes, the beach, the patch of pine trees to the north, the ancient timber holiday shacks, the rooftops of the scruffy village. Further inland, the pitheads with their winding gear, the distant moors.

"Mebbe they think it's beautiful or something."

"Beautiful!" He elbowed me. "Is that the word? Howay, let's go and introduce ourselves."

We stood up and shuffled through the sand and crossed the lighthouse headland. Daniel was at the rock pools, lifting stones, inspecting the water, putting the stones back again. He held something for a moment on his hand and we saw him smile before he put it into the water again.

"Ah," said Joseph. "Doesn't he look sweet?"

He strode across the rocks. I followed, a couple of steps behind.

"Hello, new kid," he said when he was ten feet away. "I said hello, how d'you do, nice to see you."

Daniel stood calf-deep in the clear pool, sandals in his hand. He had a loose striped T-shirt on. His skin was tanned. He held his hair back, looked at us through clear blue eyes.

"I said hello," said Joseph. "Are you deaf or daft?"

"Hello," said Daniel.

He bent down and tugged at another rock.

"Are you pestering our crabs?" said Joseph. "Poking our starfish?"

He picked up a fist-sized stone and lobbed it into Daniel's pool.

"Joseph, man," I whispered, but he took no notice.

"Leave them poor little beasts alone," he said. "What they done to you?"

Daniel didn't look at us. He stepped out of the other side of the pool and started to walk away.

"Are you a nance?" said Joseph. He sniggered. "You must be." He nudged me. "He must be! Deaf and daft and a nance."

There was a drone of engines in the sky. Daniel looked up, but it was just a plane banking over the sea before it headed into Newcastle. He looked back.

"I'm Joseph Connor!" said Joseph. "And this is me mate Bobby Burns! Watch your step, bonny lad. You'll never know when we're about."

Daniel walked on, waded homeward through the sea again.

Joseph laughed.

"What's wrong with you?" he said.

"Nowt," I answered.

"Good. He's got to learn whose place this is. Hoy!" he yelled. "Nancy boy!"

Daniel just walked on.

Joseph took a sheath knife out of his pocket, took the knife out of the sheath and held it up. He touched the point and laughed through gritted teeth.

"Howay," he said. "Let's play war."

❧ NINE ❧

We went into the pines. The earth was soft, the light was dappled. It was a place where everybody loved to play, and it was a place where lots of kids went to war. Away from the footpaths there were holes and dens and trenches. Ropes dangled from the trees, some of them with nooses at the end. Kids' names were carved into the bark. The names went ages back, back to the time my dad himself was just a kid. Ever since anybody could remember, this was where kids played out battles against the Germans or the Japanese. The pines became the Somme, the Burmese jungle, the coast of Normandy, the streets of Berlin. Kids became cowboys or American Indians and stalked each other with guns and tomahawks. They turned into Christians and Muslims slashing each other apart during the Crusades. Kids were tortured, hanged, drawn and quartered. They had their hearts ripped out by Aztec priests, they were thrown to the lions by Ancient Romans, they were bludgeoned by cave dwellers wielding clubs. Some days the place rang with cries and screams and laughter: Kill! Get him! String him up! Die, you fiend!

Joseph threw his knife and it thudded into a tree. He laughed.

"Gan on," he said. "Pull the knife out. Then try and get me."

I went to the knife, pulled it out, and suddenly he was at me, wrenching it from my hand, holding it to my throat.

"Too slow, little Bobby," he said. "I'd've had your throat cut before you knew it."

He laughed again.

"Mebbes I'll be a commando and not a builder," he said. "Travel. Adventure. War."

He stabbed the tree.

"Got ya!" he said.

We ran through the trees carrying fallen branches as if they were guns. We dropped into a trench. We peered over the edge. Through the trees we saw the people on the beach. We set up a mortar and cupped our ears as we set it off. We hunkered down and made the sounds of distant explosions. Then we peered over the edge again.

"There's still survivors," Joseph said, so we set the mortar off again.

We played an hour or so like that, dealing imaginary

death and mayhem to Keely Bay; then we sat together against the rough trunk of a pine. Joseph cleaned his knife, stabbing it time and again into the sandy earth until its blade was gleaming.

"Kid got knifed at school last term," he said. "One of the third-years. It's true," he said when he saw my amazement. "A little cheeky kid called Billy Fox. Nowt dangerous. He just got it in the arm." He put his knife back in its sheath. "Makes you think, though, eh."

We stood up and headed back.

"Slog Porter from Blyth done it. He's a cracker. Really bloody scary. It's the last we'll see of him, I hope."

Closer to the beach, the smell of chips came from the café. Joseph breathed deep.

"Bliddy lovely," he said.

He lit a cigarette.

We passed a couple lying close together behind a windbreak. Joseph nudged me. Their tinny transistor played pop, then moved on to the news. The sound faded behind us.

"Do you think there'll be another war?" I said.

"A war?"

"The Third World War. Atom bombs. The end of everything."

"Why, no," he answered. "Me dad says we've grown out of all that stuff."

In the water, some kids were squealing that they'd seen a shark.

"Mind you," said Joseph, "if there is a war, I'll be there. A commando." He lifted his knife and dived at a phantom in the sand. "Die, you fiend!"

❧ TEN ❧

I was just wiping the sauce off my mouth after lunch when I heard cart wheels rumbling in the lane outside. Ailsa and her brothers and her dad went past the window. Their ancient pony, Wilberforce, was pulling their cart. Ailsa sat in the back, on top of a heap of coal. She leaned down and peered in and saw me there and waved. Her face was nearly as black as her hair and her eyes were sparkling bright.

Mam laughed.

"Coaly scamp," she said. "Just like her mother was, God bless her soul."

Ailsa's face went out of sight, but the voice rang out.

"Bobby! Howay, help us, Bobby, man!"

I grabbed an apple and went after them and Mam yelled I'd better make sure I had a damn good wash before I came back in.

They were just a few yards past the house. Ailsa's dad and her brothers Losh and Yak were walking.

"Bobbeee!" Ailsa yelled when she saw me.

She reached out a hand and I grabbed it and Yak shoved and soon I was up there with her.

"Are you looking for work, lad?" said her dad.

"Aye," I said.

He spat out a black stream from his black face.

"Then you'll have some tanners in your pocket by teatime."

We trundled on.

"We're hoying this off," said Ailsa. "Then we're going in again."

The lane was all potholes and the wheels kept slipping and we rocked and slithered on the cold damp coal. She lay back like it was a mound of warm soft sand. I sat beside her. There were gannets and larks and gulls above us. A flock of pigeons clattered past.

"Look at this, Bobby," she said.

She dug in a pocket and brought out one half of a broken metal heart attached to a rusted chain.

She rubbed it with her fingers.

"We're always finding little treasures in the coal," she said. "Look, there's words on it."

She scraped them with a little penknife. She showed the words to me. We deciphered them together.

Without my other half I am as nothing.

She laughed.

"What a tragic little tale there could be there," she said. She put the half-heart in my hand. "Go on, it's yours. Daddy! Tell that silly Wilberforce to stop his rocking."

"Stop that rocking, horse!" her dad yelled, and we all laughed.

We came to their house, an old redbrick place with rusting lean-tos all around. There was an ancient pickup truck and heaps of coal and scrap metal. Behind the house, an allotment garden ran toward the dunes. Huge flowers were blooming there. There were onions and carrots and potatoes, all in neat straight rows. There was a greenhouse filled with gleaming red tomatoes. There was a bright blue painted pigeon loft with its doors wide open. The flock of pigeons clattered and wheeled above us. Chickens squawked and pecked in the yard.

Ailsa jumped down and ran into the house and put a kettle on the gas. I helped the men to shovel the coal from the cart. We all drank mugs of tea, standing in a group outside the back door.

"Your mam and dad OK?" said her dad.

"Aye," I said.

"Not seen him down the Rat."

"He's not been getting out much," I said.

"No? He's working, though?"

"Aye. But he's on holiday this week."

"You'll be off to the Riviera, then?"

"Mebbe. Or mebbe we'll just go to Worgate again."

"Hahaha. That's where we're ganning and all. There or Worgarden."

He swiped his fist across his lips. He glugged his tea.

"You know," he said, "there was a time it looked like that dad of yours'd be setting up in competition."

"Aye. He's told me."

We grinned. It was the tale of how in his young days Dad got himself an old pram and a shovel and a sieve and started to try to get the coal, and how it led to nothing but jokes and laughter from Ailsa's dad's lot.

"Aye," said Ailsa's dad. "They were hard days, that's the truth of it. He didn't mean no harm. And he was called up pretty soon so it came to nowt."

He kicked a chicken from under his feet.

"Tell him I've been asking," he said, and he looked me in the eye. "He's a good man, that dad of yours. And a good woman is your mam. Now then, lads. And little lass. Let's get splashing. Wilberforce! You got any life left in them bones?"

✿ ELEVEN ✿

We went to the sea. I rolled my jeans up past my knees but it was useless. In seconds I was soaked. Ailsa's dad and brothers wore ancient chest-high waders. She was bare-legged.

"Howay, man," said Yak. "Get your bliddy keks off."

So I stripped down to my pants, threw my jeans onto the sand and plunged forward into the waves. I had a battered metal sieve. I shoved it down into the sand beneath the sea, let the waves sluice through it so that the sand fell through; then I tipped the black remains onto the cart. Ailsa's dad and brothers worked further out, with huge flat spades and massive sieves. Yak and Losh kept wading back with buckets full of coal.

"Black gold!" sang Losh. "Come and buy our beautiful black gold."

"Hoy!" yelled Yak.

"Aye!" I answered.

"Why did the priest take a machine gun to church?"

"I don't know!" I yelled. "Why?"

"To make the people holy!"

Ailsa worked with me and was faster and surer than me and she moved in rhythm with the waves. She slicked her hair from her eyes with strong wet hands.

"You're doing great, Bobby boy," she shouted. "Ain't he, Daddy? Ain't Bobby doing great?"

"Aye!" laughed her dad. "A bit more time and he'll be nearly as good as his father was."

Afterward, Wilberforce pulled the cart from the sea. Losh put a head-bag full of hay on him. Seawater drained down through the coal, through the timbers of the cart, and soaked away into the sand. The men smoked. I sat on a stone beside Ailsa.

"Joseph reckons you'll not be coming into school," I said.

She threw her head back.

"Him!"

"He reckons you might just try to go to his place."

"What does he know?"

I shoved my toes down into the sand.

"You going to go anywhere?" I said.

"I might and I mightn't," she answered.

"You got your uniform?" I said.

"Uniform!"

Yak was watching and listening and grinning.

"What's the point of it?" he said.

"The point of what?" I said.

"What's the point of lasses learning?" he said.

I shrugged, couldn't say anything.

"See?" he said. "No point at all. All they need is a canny lad with a bit of brawn and a bit of brain and a mind to make a bob or two."

He whistled, pondered, and gazed into the sky.

"I wonder," he said. "Is there any takers?"

Then he and Losh rushed at us and lifted us up and threw us into the turning waves and I thrashed my arms and gasped for breath and blew out water and swam back to the shore at Ailsa's side and we lay there hooting and laughing on the sand, and it was wonderful.

🎞 TWELVE 🎞

"They're teachers," said Mam. "That's the story. At the university, they say."

"University!" said Dad.

"And there's a daughter, but she's traveling. It's all a bit vague. She's called Pat and he's called Paul."

The three of us were at the window, looking out. Daniel and his parents were on the beach.

"And Paul's got a brother that's an actor."

"Hm!" said Dad. He lit a cigarette and coughed.

"He's on the telly sometimes. He was on *Emergency Ward 10* last week."

Paul had a camera. He kept taking photographs—not of his family, but of the place. He pointed it toward our house and moved toward us and we moved back.

"And Daniel'll be at school with you, Bobby. They were seen buying the blazer at Raymond Barnes."

"You spoken to him yet?" said Dad.

I shook my head.

"He might make a nice pal for you," said Mam.

She clicked her tongue.

"Put that out," she said to Dad.

He rolled his eyes, but took a final drag and threw his cigarette into the cold grate. He coughed and swallowed.

"What's he up to now?" he said.

Paul was standing with his legs apart and the camera to his face again.

"What on earth's he think he's seeing?" said Mam. She slicked her hair down. She laughed. "I'd've washed the windows if I'd known."

Paul took his photograph, then turned away, with the camera slung over his shoulder, and his hands in his pockets. The sky was huge and blue and empty: just the sun, the gulls, the pigeons. There was a trawler a half mile out, with gulls all around it, plunging for waste.

Mam put her arm around me and kissed me.

"That's for nothing," she said. "Now get out from under me feet and let me get on."

"Howay," said Dad. "Something to show you. That feller's just put it in me mind."

We went up onto the landing. He opened the door of the high cupboard. He stood on tiptoes but couldn't reach the top shelf, so he put his arms around my thighs and lifted me.

"You're looking for a black book," he said. "That old

album thing. Remember? God knows where it is. Shove your hand under them blankets."

I rested on his shoulder and slid my hand in. There were boxes and tins and lumpy parcels.

"Like a book," he said. "Thick. Somewhere in there, I'm sure."

I pulled a square cardboard box out to clear my way.

"Bugger," he said. "We still got them things? Hoy that down and all."

I slid my hand further in, felt a book, dragged it. He saw its edge.

"Aye," he said. "Good lad. That's the one."

❊ THIRTEEN ❊

He opened them in my room, by the window. The cardboard box was first. It had a gas mask inside.

"Thought we'd chucked these out years ago," he said. "Here, give us your head."

It was black rubber, with straps to go around your head and with thick glass lenses for your eyes. There was a long snout-shaped piece that covered your nose and mouth and that had a metal filter at its end. He rubbed the lenses with his fingertips. He stretched the straps over my head and they caught in my hair and tugged. He pulled the snout over my face. I gasped. I had to suck for breath. The air that came was fusty and ancient. I goggled out through the cloudy lenses at his grinning face. My face suddenly grew hot. I sucked for breath again. I ripped the straps from my head and ripped strands of hair away with them. I pulled the snout away and opened my mouth wide and breathed.

"Aye," he said. "Not much fun, eh?"

He weighed the mask in his hand, remembering.

"Every living soul had one of these," he said. "Young and old, big and small. No one moved without one. We lived in fear and dread. When they coming? What they going to do to us? Then nothing happened, then we got used to it. Then they did start coming, and the bombs did start falling. There was no gas, though. Not that. Not the worst things we'd imagined."

Then he put the mask back down and pulled the book to us. When he started to turn the pages I knew I had seen them before, years ago.

"I been saying for yonks I'll sort these out," he said. "Look at the blinking state of them."

The photographs had come away from their thin mountings. They slid out from between the pages. All of them were black-and-white. All of them were faded. There he was, my dad as a little boy on the beach in wellingtons and shorts and a scruffy vest and a leaping mongrel at his side. There he was with Joseph Connor's dad, both of them kneeling by a smoking fire in the pines with bows and arrows in their hands and with seagull feathers in their hair. There he was with Ailsa's dad, teenaged and thin and hungry-looking, perched by the rock pools, smoking.

"But these aren't the ones," he said, moving on, turning a sheaf of pages until there he was again, in his army kit, cocking his thumb for the photographer with the jungle behind him and the Burmese sun beating down.

He sighed.

"A lad called Jackie Marr from Shields took that one," he said. "That very morning a sniper's bullet went straight through his poor heart. Ah, well..." He turned the page. He grinned. "Now look at this, son."

Now I saw them, I remembered these as well: the snake charmer who played his pipes while a cobra rose from the basket between his feet; the little naked boy climbing away from a bunch of soldiers up a rope that seemed attached to nothing but empty air; the ancient turbaned man lying on his bed of nails in a seething marketplace; and then the wild man with painted stripes on his face, who glared full-face into the camera and had a sword stuck through his face from cheek to cheek.

"Just like McNulty!" I said.

"Aye. Just like McNulty. There were lots of them in those wild days. Fakes and fakirs and magic men. Dervishes and quacks. Miracle makers. We found them in the markets, on the roadsides, at the frontiers. Mebbe it was all the wars and disturbances that brung them out. And mebbe there was them among them that could work true magic and make true miracles come to pass. But poor souls like McNulty sat at their feet while the sun glared down and the bullets rattled and the bayonets stabbed and the bombs fell and the sun blazed down and the skin got scorched and the brain got melted and the heart got broke. This is where McNulty comes from, son. From a mad mad time before your time, from a time of bloody blasted war."

He opened my window, lit a cigarette.

"And I was there as well," he said. "And for one as old as me it's not so long ago, and it drove us all a little mad and a little sad and left us all with partly broken hearts."

He breathed smoke out into the air above the lane. He reached out and stroked my face.

"Must seem another age to you," he said.

"Aye," I said, and it did: so far away, so long ago.

The light was falling. I switched the Lourdes light on. I looked down at the black-and-white boys on the beach and in the pines, at the magic men. The photographs were like windows into ancient places. And my dad had been there. He read my thoughts.

"It'll be different for you," he said. "You can do anything. You can go anywhere. The world is yours. You're privileged and free."

We both turned our faces to the sky.

"As long as there's no war," he said. "As long as there's no more of that stupidity."

I reached into my pocket and touched the broken heart.

"Please, God," I said inside myself. "No more bombs, no more wars."

"Please, God," said Dad. He put the gas mask back into its box, touched Mary's halo, then put his arm around me. "We can't be that stupid. Not again."

❊ FOURTEEN ❊

I nearly bumped into him behind the beach café. I was out thinking I'd find Joseph. We nearly hit each other but we swayed apart. He looked at me, then dropped his gaze.

"Oh," he said. "It's you."

"Aye."

He started moving on.

"Joseph's all right," I said quickly.

"Is he?"

"He likes to be tough, that's all."

"Or stupid," he muttered.

I took a step toward him.

"What do you mean?"

He shrugged.

"Nothing."

He started to move on again.

"We'll be going to the same school," I said.

"Will we?"

"Aye. Yes."

"Sacred Heart."

"Yes."

He tapped his foot on the café wall, knocking sand and coal out of his sandals.

"Me name's Bobby," I said. "Robert."

"Is it?" he said.

"Yes. And you're Daniel."

He rolled his eyes.

"That's good to know," he said.

"I live back there, look. That one."

"Do you?"

"Yes."

I was about to tell him where he lived, but I didn't. We looked at each other.

"Have you been here long?" he said.

"Forever."

"That's long."

The pigeons clattered over us.

"It's OK here," I said. "Some say it's the back of beyond, but..."

"That's what my dad says. But he says that's why he likes it. He's thinking about making a book about it."

"What kind of book?"

"Photographs. He says he wants to catch it before it changes." He regarded me. "Maybe he'll put you in the book."

"Me?"

I tried to imagine a book with me in it. Me playing in the pines with Joseph. Me standing in the sea with Ailsa. Me sitting by the fire with my mam and dad.

"He's a lecturer," Daniel said. "He does history of art at the university. My mum does English." He smiled. "What do your parents do?"

"Me dad's a fitter in the yard."

"The yard?"

"The shipyard. It's at Blyth. It's a little one for little ships. Little trawlers, tugs, that kind of thing. He's on holiday just now."

"And your mum?"

"Me mam?"

"Yes."

I shrugged.

"Dunno," I said. "Looks after us and that."

We stood there, like we wondered was there anything else to say. I looked at his striped T-shirt. There was a badge on the heart side with a symbol on it. He saw me looking and held it with his fingers.

"CND," he said.

"I know," I lied.

"It's the Campaign for Nuclear Disarmament."

"I know," I lied.

"Do you keep up with things?" he said. "With current affairs, world events?"

"Dunno," I said.

He looked at the sea. Dark clouds were heaping up on the horizon.

"When does it get really cold?" he said.

"Eh?"

"It's the North. We thought it'd be winter already but it's not, is it?"

"It'll come."

I thought of the winds that would lash at their big new windows, the waves that would crash within yards of it. I thought of whirling sleet and snow and hail and sand. I thought of the ice that once came to settle on everything, even the beach, even the fringes of the sea.

"We came from Kent," he said.

"The Garden of England."

"That's right. I didn't want to come but we had to."

"We read about it in the juniors. Hops and orchards and a long growing season."

"It's beautiful. I don't suppose you've been there."

"No."

"Have you traveled?"

"Me dad's been to Burma. And me mam's been to Lourdes."

"Ah."

"She saw a man cured there. He'd been on crutches for ten years. He threw them away."

"Did he really?"

"Aye. It was a miracle."

We were silent again; then he shrugged and continued

on his way. I measured myself against him as he passed. I clenched my fists. I wondered how I'd do if I ever had to fight him.

"See you," I said.

"Yes," he answered. "I'll see you."

🎋 FIFTEEN 🎋

One night that week I woke in the dead hours. Couldn't sleep. Prayers and hymns were running through my head. I switched the Lourdes light on. I put McNulty's silver coin there, and the tanners from Ailsa's dad. Mary looked down on Bernadette and on these offerings below her. I tore out a page from my notebook. I put Ailsa's broken heart on it and drew the other half of the heart so that it looked healed. I drew a CND symbol on another page. I wrote the words:

Please. Do not let us be so stupid. Never again. Amen.

I folded the page into quarters and tucked it under the lamp.

I opened the window and breathed the sea and the night. Nothing moved against the stars.

What was the sound that mingled with the turning waves? The voices of wailing sailors? The whistling of breath in Dad's throat? Jazz?

"Please," I whispered.

In the room next door, Dad started coughing.

I left the light on. I lay down again. Dad went on coughing; I gazed into Mary's face.

"Please," I whispered. "Never again."

Dad stopped. We slept in peace.

❧ SIXTEEN ❧

That Sunday Dad and I went to early Mass together; then we waited outside the Rat. We ate the bread and hard-boiled eggs we'd brought to break our fast. It was a cold, white morning. Dad had his heavy brown herring-bone coat on. We heard a hooting and whistling and creaking of wings and then a flight of geese appeared below the clouds, flying southward in a great wide V.

"They're leaving early," said Dad. "Mebbe they smelt something coming on the wind."

Soon the bus came and we sat at the back and rattled toward Newcastle. I crossed my fingers, hoping that McNulty would be there again.

"Will he recognize you?" I said.

"Who knows? It was a long time back. And I don't think he recognized me even then."

He smiled.

"More likely he'll know you, son—his bright assistant from just a week ago."

We came to the city's heart. We got out by the monument, below the angel. Dad nodded a greeting to the stone soldiers and the names as we walked by.

"Angels!" he hissed.

"Angels?"

"I saw no angels, Bobby. I saw nothing leaning down to help. All I saw was struggle and pain and young lives blighted. Bloody war's got nowt to do with angels!"

The stillness and silence of a Sunday hung over everything. Quiet streets. Nothing open. Newspaper sellers stood at the street corners. On the front page of the *People*, matched photos of Kennedy and Khrushchev stared out with a fake tear in between. A WORLD TORN IN HALF, the headline said. A few buses, hardly any cars. Many pedestrians like us were heading down toward the quay. Our heels clacked and echoed on the pavements.

"It's cold enough," said Dad, and he shuddered, and pulled his overcoat close as an icy drizzle started.

We followed the steep downward curve of Dean Street. High buildings of blackened stone loomed over us. There were archways and dark stone stairways cut into them: Dog Leap Stairs, Break Neck Stairs, the Black Gate, Amen Corner. Beyond them, St. Nicholas' bells began to ring.

We turned the final curve. Clouds rested on the high

arch of the bridge. Hidden seagulls squealed. Steam and smoke rose from the stalls. The river was swollen, oily-looking, seemed hardly to move.

We paused at a joke stall and laughed at the fake boils and warts, the monkey masks, the nails that could appear to pierce fingers, the packets of fart powders, bottles of smells. We walked on and a Gypsy came to us and showed us a twist of paper in her cracked palm.

"A cure for all ills," she whispered.

She opened the paper, showed the seeds and broken leaves inside.

"Take it, sir," she said. "It was picked by a Gypsy beneath a full moon."

I moved away, but Dad hesitated. She touched his hand.

"It cures the blood, the breath, the skin, the eye, the brain," she said. "It heals the heart."

She held him.

"Name your illness, sir."

He shook his head. She placed the twist of paper in his hand.

"Take it, sir."

He licked his lips, shrugged and passed a coin to her.

"Thank you, sir," she said. She looked into my eye. "You will be lucky in love," she said. "And that's for nothing."

She turned and went away.

Dad put the mixture in his pocket. He looked down.

"Always the same, eh?" he muttered. He tried to grin. "You can never get away from them, eh?"

He lit a cigarette. We twisted our way between the stalls. We laughed at the ancient bearded man swigging cider, who carried the sandwich board:

REPENT. THE DARKNESS IS BUT A BREATH AWAY.

We saw no audience, we heard no voice demanding that we pay.

"Mebbe he's moved on," said Dad. "Mebbe he was only passing through."

Then we saw the plume of fire leaping upward beneath the bridge.

"Or mebbe he's come back," said Dad.

The fire leapt again.

"This way," said Dad, and we walked toward the flame.

❧ SEVENTEEN ❧

"It's really him," breathed Dad. "Who'd believe it, after all these years?"

I teetered on tiptoes and tried to see through the crowd. Dad lifted me up. There he was, below the bridge, half naked and eyes blazing as before. He had a pair of burning torches. He ran them back and forward across his skin. He sipped from a bottle, breathed across a torch, and the fire leapt from his lips. The air was filled with the stench of fire and paraffin.

He ran the flames across his skin again.

"Who could dare to touch the fire?" he snarled. "Who could dare to eat the flames? Who could dare such madness?"

He plunged a torch into his mouth and extinguished it. He plunged the other torch into his mouth and extinguished it. He opened his mouth and gasped smoke.

He lit the torches again. He breathed fire again, a great high spreading flag of it.

"Lethal," whispered Dad.

I looked at him.

"There's many lost a lung, many lost a life from fire-eating. Breathe in when you should be breathing out and..."

McNulty glared. He roared. He held the torches at arm's length and turned his face to the sky. He ran the torches swiftly across himself.

"In the greatest of the fire-eaters," he said, "you cannot see where the fire ends and the man begins."

He plunged the torches into his mouth and drew them out again, still burning.

He looked at us, more gentle.

"Pay," he said. "What would you pay for such a feast? What would you pay to let McNulty do these things? Pay! Get your money out and pay."

He swallowed the flames and put the torches out. He pushed his stick and sack at the crowd. Many dropped coins in, many backed away. Many sniggered and twisted their faces and shook their heads.

"What's next?" he called. "The chains or the needles? More fire? Are we ready for more fire?"

He saw me, perched there over Dad's shoulder. He narrowed his eyes, pondered, as if trying to remember me. He pushed his way toward us, demanding and gathering coins. He shoved the sack at us. Dad dropped a coin in. I slithered down from Dad's shoulder.

"Hello, bonny," said McNulty.

"Hello," I softly said.

"There was an angel at your side," he said. "I remember. All done up in red."

"Me mam. She's at home."

"That's good. Me mam wrapped up safe and warm at home," he said. He looked at Dad, looked away. He hugged himself. "These is days of bitter cold. You noticed that, my bonny?"

"Aye."

"You hear the whispers on the water?" he said. "You hear the thunder in the skies?"

I shook my head.

"Then it's mebbes nowt. Just McNulty and his great bamboozlement."

He leaned close to my ear. He cupped his hand about my shoulder. Dad held me too, and others gathered close, trying to listen to this meeting between the fire-eater and the boy, but it was as if there were just the two of us lost together there on the quay.

"Oh, bonny," he whispered. "Just watch and listen and hear the slapping of the water and the tolling of the bell."

"It's just the river and the mist and a warning bell."

"Hear the thundering deep inside the clouds."

"It's just an airplane, Mr. McNulty."

He caught his breath, closed his eyes, tilted his head, peeped out again. He leaned close, as if I could listen to the noises in his head.

"Hear the yelling and rampaging deep inside my skull."

"I hear nothing, Mr. McNulty."

"Is that true? There's nowt outside? Just peace and quiet? Mebbe it's so. Mebbe McNulty's just too much alone, my bonny boy, and he needs a lad like you to be beside him. Come and help us, bonny. Come and open that box for us again."

"McNulty," said Dad.

McNulty's eyes swiveled toward him.

"Do you remember me?" said Dad.

No answer.

"We were in Burma, McNulty," he said. "We came back on the boat together."

"I remember nowt," said McNulty. "I remember that days is light and nights is dark and that the year turns round us like a wheel." He jabbed his sack at Dad's chest. "Money out and pay."

Dad dropped a coin into the sack.

"We were in Burma," he said. "We were in the war, McNulty. When we went out, we were hardly more than lads. When we came back—"

"I remember nowt. There was days of fiery heat and now there's days of icy cold. I was young and now I'm old. I remember this boy was a help to me and there was an angel at his side and I hear the booming and the thundering in the skies. Help us again, bonny?"

"I helped you," said Dad. "Remember? You were on the stairs. They'd beaten you."

"Look at this one," said McNulty.

He ran his hand across the picture of a woman tattooed on his upper arm.

THERESA was written under it. TRUE FOREVER.

"Who's this?" he hissed. "I look at her and look at her and get no answer." He rubbed the ink as if trying to rub it away. "Who's this? How did this get on us?" He touched the other tattoos. "And this one, and this one. Where did these come from?"

He reached to me again. He cupped my face in his fingers. His body stank of kerosene and fire.

"I'm like a little bairn. I remember nowt. I know that you were here with us before, and there was an angel all in red, but past that there's just darkness and silence and a great nowtness, going on forever." He sniffed. "I smell fish and salt on you, bonny."

"The sea. We live beside it. Keely Bay."

"Lucky boy. Don't get on them boats, though."

"And you," said Dad. "Where do you live, McNulty?"

"On the ground."

"Where do you sleep?"

"On the ground. In holes, in doorways and alleyways. In the dark where nobody passes. And I wander."

He kissed me quickly on the cheek.

"The sea," he said. "Mebbes one day I'll come wandering past your place. Keep your eyes peeled. Listen out for us."

He looked at our audience. He glared. They shrank away. They laughed. He jabbed his sack at them. He moved away from us. Dad caught at his elbow and he turned and looked into Dad's eyes and there was a yearning in him, as if he wanted to stay with us, talk with us, as if he wanted to stop being McNulty with his stick and sack and his instruments of torture. But he broke away. He hurried to his wheel. He lifted it to his knees. He lifted it into the sky and rested it on his skull and he stamped the earth as he bore its weight and teetered and searched for a place of balance. Soon the wheel thudded back down to the cobblestones and it shattered when it fell.

"Poor soul," said Dad.

And McNulty was lost in himself again. He wept over the broken wheel. Then he opened his box. He took the skewer out. He shoved it through his cheeks. He grunted and hissed and his eyes were filled with fight and fire.

❊ EIGHTEEN ❊

Next morning I put the uniform on. I put a new leather satchel on my back. Mam could hardly speak. Dad just shook his head and grinned.

"Who'd believe it?" he said. "Who'd blinking believe it?"

I rolled my eyes.

"All I did was get older," I said. "All I'm doing is starting a new school."

He clapped his hands and Mam spoke through her tears at last.

"Yes, we know," she said. "It's nothing. It's ordinary. And it's just miraculous."

They came out with me. They watched me from the front door as I walked along the lane beside the beach. Seagulls squealed and the sea slapped and a foghorn droned from beyond the lost horizon. I waved once, then turned into the lane toward the Rat. I kept pulling the loose blazer up to my shoulders. My brightly polished shoes were stiff. The shirt collar chafed my throat. One of Mam's tacking pins was still in the blazer cuff. I pulled it out and stuck it in a seam. I shivered and my heart raced.

"Bobby! Bobby!"

I couldn't tell where it came from. Then there was a wolf whistle, and my name was called again.

"Bobby! Little Bobby Burns!"

There he was, backed into a hawthorn shrub. Joseph. He came out as I passed. His voice was high and singsong, like a girl's.

"Ooh, Bobby," he said. "Don't you look so sweet?"

He came to my side, walked at my side. He tapped a finger at his cheek; he raised his eyebrows.

"So, Robert. Do you think it will be mathematics this morning? Or geography? Art history, of course. Or perhaps there will be flower-sniffing. Do you have your dancing shoes today? There will of course be elocution. How now, brown cow? Where does the rain in Spain fall, Robert?"

I walked and let him talk. I kept my eyes averted.

"On the plain, of course," he said. "On the blasted plain."

He smiled. He put his arm around my shoulders.

"Just kidding," he said. "You know that, eh?"

"Aye."

"Aye. Good lad." He licked his lips. "I'm proud of you, Bobby."

He turned his eyes away. We walked in silence, close to each other.

"Done you this," he muttered.

He pushed a little penknife into my hand.

"It's nowt," he said.

I held it in my palm: a black stock, a shining silver blade.

"It's nowt," he said again. "Just something I had in me box."

"It's great," I said.

His face colored and he shrugged.

"Thanks," I said.

We didn't know what else to say. We saw Daniel coming out of his own lane, walking in his new uniform toward the Rat.

"Look at the way he walks," said Joseph. "Like he's a bloody tart. Like he owns the bloody place. Know what I mean?"

"Aye."

"Keep your distance from him, eh?"

"I will."

He gripped my shoulders and squeezed me with his strong hands.

"Good luck, Bobby," he said. "You're a special kid."

Then he turned and hurried back through the hawthorn hedge.

I watched him leave my sight.

I ran my fingers across the letters he'd carved into the bone handle: BOBBY.

✥ NINETEEN ✥

We nodded at each other, but I didn't sit with Daniel on the bus. He sat behind me and my cheeks were burning. I thought he was watching me, but when I dared to turn I saw he was reading a book, lounging with his knee raised onto the seat. He had his tie loosened and he held his hair back with his hand. I turned back again when he raised his eyes to me. Other kids got on, older kids, but some of my mates from the juniors as well: Ed Garbutt, Diggy Hare, Col O'Kane. Diggy sat beside me, the other two in front.

"They stick your head down the netty, you know," he said. "They turn you upside down and pull the chain. Initiation."

"Aye, I know," said Col. "I heard. D'you sometimes wish you hadn't passed?"

"Aye," we all muttered.

"Who's that?" said Ed, nodding at Daniel.

"New kid," I said. "Come from Kent or somewhere."

"They make you eat dirt," said Diggy. "They make you drink your own piss. They stick needles in you. They got one kid took to hospital and he nearly died. It's true. Johnny Murray told us."

"I heard the same," said Col. "They had to pump his guts out and he's never been the same since."

A couple of the older kids were grinning at us. We kept our eyes away. Doreen Armstrong got on. Her skirt was hitched up above her knees.

"Oh, wow," said Col.

"D'you sometimes wish you were older?" said Ed.

"Aye," we muttered.

We headed down the coast. The sea was on our left. A massive tanker was heading in toward the Tyne. Some kind of battleship was heading out into the mist.

"Me dad nearly didn't let us come," said Ed. "Says it's hardly worth the bother. Says what's the point in all the tests and the uniform palaver. Says there's bound to be another war and when there is . . ."

I shook my head.

"There won't be," I said.

"How d'you know?" said Col.

I shook my head.

"See?" said Ed. "Nobody knows. Nobody can do nowt."

"There'll be nowt left," said Diggy. "They could blow the whole world up umpteen times if they wanted to."

"Kapow," said Col.

"They hung one kid," said Diggy. "They did. If the teacher hadn't come along and cut him down . . ."

"But they say the teachers is even worse," said Col.

I felt the penknife in my pocket. I opened the blade.

"I was in town yesterday, at the quayside market," I said. "I saw this fire-eater bloke."

"Me and all," said Ed. "He's a bliddy loony, eh?"

"Aye," I said.

I felt the sharpness of the blade against my thumb.

One of the big kids lit a cigarette at the back of the bus. Doreen squealed with laughter at a joke. Ed put his chin on the seat back and stared at Daniel. Diggy looked out at the sea.

"It's like ganning to the bliddy slaughterhouse," said Col.

❧ TWENTY ❧

There was a long redbrick front with long shining windows. There was a great golden crucifix over the main door. Half a dozen steps led up to it. We first-years had to wait there when the bell had rung. The others streamed inside. A group of teachers stood on the steps above us.

"Your names will be called," said one. "Then you will step forward. When your class has been gathered, your teacher will escort you inside."

He had a suit and tie on, and a black gown over his suit. He drew his gown open. A black leather strap curled out from his breast pocket.

"My name is Mr. Todd," he said. "Your teachers will introduce themselves when they are with you in your rooms." He paused. "We are waiting for order."

He came closer to us.

"I wish to see straight lines," he said. "Straight lines!"

We made clumsy lines that straggled out across the pale concrete yard.

He sighed.

"So," he said. "You are those who have passed the eleven-plus. You are the elite." His face hardened. "Do not believe it. You may have proved that you have something like a brain. But you have not yet proved that you are suitable to be with us. You have not proved that you have character or moral fiber. You are half civilized. You are wild things. And you must be taught to conform."

I kept turning, trying to see Ailsa, but she was nowhere.

"What is your name?"

He was at my side. He held the strap between his hands.

"What is your name?" he said again.

"R-Robert Burns."

"Robert Burns what?"

"Robert Burns, sir."

"Put your hand out, Robert Burns."

I blinked.

"Put your hand out."

I put my hand out. He raised the strap as high as his shoulder and lashed it across my palm.

"Other hand," he said. "Other hand!"

I put out my other hand. He strapped me again. I clenched my stinging hands. Tears burned the rims of my eyes.

"You will pay attention when a teacher speaks," he said. "Do you understand?"

I couldn't answer. He flexed the strap.

"Do you understand?"

"Yes."

"Yes what?"

"Yes, sir."

"Yes, sir. I have my eye on you, Robert Burns. I know you now."

He moved on. I heard kids gasping for breath around me. I kept my eyes to the front. The other teachers looked down on us, expressionless.

Todd said it again. I didn't turn.

"What is your name, boy?"

"Daniel Gower." He said it calmly, confidently. "Sir," he added.

"What is this, Gower?"

"It is my hair. Sir."

"It is too long."

There was silence. Then Todd spoke again.

"No boy looks at me like that. Put your hand out. Put your hand out!"

I flinched as the strap struck Daniel's hand, as it struck his other hand.

"You will have your hair cut," said Todd. "You will never again look at a teacher like that."

He moved to the front again. He held a file of names.

"Many of you will find that you are separated from

those you knew before. This is not a play group or a happy family. When your name is called, step forward."

He began the roll call of the names. I was separated from Diggy, Col and Ed. Ailsa's name was called and nobody stepped forward. My name was in the same group as Daniel's. As we moved forward together, he squeezed my arm.

"He's an evil bastard," he hissed.

We sat close together in the classroom that was filled with single desks. Our teacher, Lubbock, sat before us.

"Some of us have begun to be taught our lessons early," he said.

He showed his teeth in a half-smile.

"It's not too bad a place once we've settled you in," he said.

He taught us how to rise and say good morning when he or another member of staff entered the room. He gave out exercise books. He laid his strap on the desk in front of him.

"Put your hands together," he said.

I pressed my palms against each other, trying to press away the last of the pain.

"We will say the Lord's Prayer," he said.

❧ TWENTY-ONE ❧

Ailsa giggled at the chicken that pecked around her feet. She picked pea pods and put them into a white enamel bowl. She kept moving away from me.

"Stop pestering me, Bobby Burns," she said.

"But why weren't you at school?" I asked her. "You must be stupid, man."

"I know." She laughed. "I know, I know. I always was."

"I don't mean that. You're really clever, man."

"I know that and all!"

I kicked the sandy soil.

"Dad left school at twelve," she said. "Losh and Yak were expelled. So mebbe it's just the family way."

She led me to the far end of the garden, where there was a fence half buried in the dunes. We sat on an ancient white-painted bench. I helped her to shell the peas. We looked out over their house toward the distant city. We could see the cranes, the steeples, the first of the tower blocks.

"Anyway," she said. "They work that hard, and they need somebody to look after them. What's it like, anyway?"

"It's OK."

She laughed.

"Aye. I'll bet."

"Some of them's Nazis," I said.

"I can imagine."

She popped a pea into my mouth, delicious and sweet.

"It's fine for you, Bobby," she said. "But I don't need it. Daddy says the coal'll last forever, even after all the pits is closed. We've got a place, we'll make a living. I love it here. I don't want nowt else."

We went on shelling peas.

"You'll leave, though," she said. "You'll go somewhere really fancy, won't you? University, all that kind of stuff."

"Will I?"

"You know you will, Bobby."

I tried to imagine all those years ahead, leaving home, going to another town. University. Nobody I knew had ever been to university.

"But you could, too," I said.

She laughed.

"Me? A sea coaler's daughter? A Spink at university!"

"You should be proud of who you are and where you come from."

She popped another pea into my mouth.

"Oh, I am, Bobby," she said. "Mebbe that's why I want to stay who I am and where I am."

I turned my face from her. I listened to the sea beyond the dunes. I thought of the waves pouring in and pouring in as they had forever.

"They'll come for you," I said.

"Who will?"

"The council. They won't let you stay away from school."

"They've been already. Daddy just told them to hadaway and shite."

We laughed together.

"But they'll be back," I said.

"Let them see if we care."

She stood up and set off back toward the house.

"Anyway," she said. "School, university, all that stupid stuff. Yuck! There's more important things."

"Like what?"

"Like miracles. Do you believe in miracles?"

"Eh?"

"You're supposed to, you lot. Howay. Come and see."

❧ TWENTY-TWO ❧

She put the bowl of peas on a bench inside the door. She took me around to the back of the house. There was a wooden shed there.

"It is a miracle," she said. "Be quiet." She smiled. "It's lovely, Bobby."

She carefully inched open the door. She crouched, low to the earth. She made soothing noises with her breath. "Hello," she whispered. At first I saw nothing, then there it was, curled up on a little bed of straw. It was a fawn, no bigger than a baby. Its eyes glowed, reflecting the daylight that fell through the dusty window above it. There was a bowl of milk beside its head.

"It was dead," she whispered. She looked me in the eye as if she was testing if I believed her. "I found it in the yard yesterday morning. Like a fox had been at it, or a dog or something. Like it had run here, been chased here, and they got it here. Wasn't breathing. Heart wasn't beating. Dead."

I touched its soft coat with the back of my hand. I felt its warmth, its little beating heart. It didn't seem to be scared. I put milk on my finger and touched its tongue. It licked gently.

"Daddy said bury the poor thing," she said. "But I couldn't. I put it in a basket beside me bed. I put a blanket on it. I told God to heal it. I stayed awake for ages, long after Daddy and the lads were fast asleep. I just kept telling God to heal it. I stroked it. I told it that I loved it. Nothing happened. And I fell asleep, and all night I dreamed of it running through fields and woods and the sun was shining bright. Then I woke up in the morning and it had its eyes open and it was looking up at me."

She stroked it with both hands.

"Isn't it so beautiful?" she said.

"Aye."

"Yak said deer play possum sometimes. Daddy said we must've been mistook. But I don't think we were. It was dead and it came alive again."

I let it lick more milk from my fingers.

"D'you believe me, Bobby?" she said.

I felt its wet tongue on my skin. I looked into its trusting eyes.

"Aye," I said.

"That's good."

She lifted the fawn into her arms and stood up and carried it out through the door.

"You got to believe, don't you?" she said. "Or nowt'd ever happen. Nowt worthwhile."

She set it on the ground outside and we watched it rise and totter on its skinny legs.

"Go on," we said. "Go on, little'n."

She giggled.

"I'll keep it here till it's strong," she said. "Then I'll put it back into the wild."

The sun fell on the fawn, its dappled fur, its dark eyes, its skinny legs. So beautiful.

"What I don't understand is why it's so young," said Ailsa.

She looked over the fields, past the pitheads, toward the distant woodlands where it must have come from.

"How d'you mean?" I said.

"It's so late, Bobby. It should've been born in spring, not now when the days are getting darker and colder."

She clicked her tongue and shook her head and smiled. She whispered into its ear:

"What were your parents thinking of?"

Then she lifted it up and put it back in the shed to protect it from the fox.

"There's no good in dead things, is there?" she said. "Best keep lovely things like this alive."

❧ TWENTY-THREE ❧

I dreamed of McNulty's fire. I dreamed that he stood on the quayside at Newcastle and breathed the fire into the air and it did not stop. It spread all around, engulfing the market stalls, the cranes, the warehouses, the arching bridge, and there was nothing but the great roar of the flames and the screams of those who'd been taken. The river became a river of fire that raced toward the sea and flames a mile high leapt from the water and the smoke blotted out the sun. I stood with Mam and Dad at our window and we had gas masks on and we saw the fire rushing toward us and there seemed nothing we could do and nowhere we could run to and we just held each other tight and then I screamed: "Breathe, Mr. McNulty! Breathe back in!" And the fire paused, and rushed away again, back to the quayside and into McNulty's throat.

Then I woke and the night was so still, so quiet.

The lighthouse light swept through my room. Dad snored next door. I knelt at the window and looked out past the Lourdes light. The beach was so calm beneath the stars. Rock pools lay like scattered glass and the sea like a great mirror. I closed my eyes against the returning lighthouse light. I tried to pray but I didn't know what to pray to and the things I whispered seemed so childish.

"Look after us. Don't let terrible things happen."

I opened my eyes. The universe went on forever and forever and it was so empty and so silent and I seemed so useless. I lifted the half-heart given to me by Ailsa and held it in my palm.

"Look after the fawn," I whispered. "Don't let it die."

I went back to bed.

I sighed and said what I knew I should say.

"Forgive Todd. Forgive Lubbock."

But I knew that was useless too, because I hated them too much.

I fell asleep again at last.

"Hello, bonny," said McNulty. I smelt the fire on his breath. "Come and help me, bonny boy."

❦ TWENTY-FOUR ❦

We sat on stools at wooden benches in the biology room. All around us were pictures of animals opened up, with their muscles and hearts and lungs all exposed. Glass jars in glass cases held tapeworms and frogs and lizards. There was a story that somewhere in the school there was a human fetus, preserved like these animals in formaldehyde, but only sixth-formers were allowed to see. Above the door as in every room, Christ hung in agony on his cross.

The teacher was a little gentle woman called Miss Bute. She tapped on her desk. She said she was going to teach us about pain. She put us into pairs. I was with Daniel. I had to draw the outline of my hand on white paper. I had to lay my hand on the desk in front of Daniel and close my eyes. Daniel had a needle. He had to touch the back of my hand with the needle. I had to say yes whenever I felt the needle. He had to mark the results on the outline of my hand. A cross showed where I had felt the needle's touch. A circle showed where he had touched me with the needle but I had felt nothing. When I opened my eyes I saw that there were many places where I had felt nothing at all.

"It is a map of pain," said Miss Bute. "There are places where you could almost draw blood and nothing would be felt. And there are places where the gentlest touch produces pain."

We had to change. Now I had the needle. Daniel had to close his eyes. I touched his hand, listened to his answers, marked his map of pain. All around us there were giggles and gasps and anguished cries.

"Now then," Miss Bute kept saying. "Act your age, children. Please settle down."

Catherine Wilkes yelled that she was bleeding. Dom Carney and Tex Wilson started to fight.

I marked Daniel's reponses on the outline of his hand. I started to tell him about McNulty, how he could touch fire, how he could push a whole skewer through himself.

"I saw him do it," I said. "In Newcastle."

"It's mind over matter," Daniel said. "You can control anything if you put your mind to it."

There was a crash and screams of laughter as Tex Wilson fell off his stool.

"Children!" yelled Miss Bute. "This is not what I expect from you! Stop what you—"

Todd came in from the corridor with his strap in his hand. There was silence. Todd looked coldly at Miss Bute.

"What are you learning?" he asked us.

No one spoke.

He prodded Geraldine Pease with the strap.

"What are you learning?" he said.

"About pain, sir," said Geraldine.

A cold grin spread over Todd's face.

"How appropriate," he murmured. "Who are the ringleaders of the disturbance, Miss Bute?"

Miss Bute looked back at him.

"It was not obvious, Mr. Todd," she said.

He sighed. His cold gaze swept across us.

"Miss Bute is a young teacher," he said. "It is your job to be good to her."

"Thank you, Mr. Todd," she said. "I am sure that things are now calm enough for me to..."

He waved her words aside.

"And it is my job to protect her," he said. He smiled. "Do you understand the ancient theory of sacrifice, children?"

No one answered.

"It is that one—or two, perhaps—must be made to suffer for the good of all." He paused. "Any volunteers?" He waited. He smiled. "Ah, well. Then I must choose."

He pointed with his strap.

"I will take you."

It was Tex Wilson.

"And you."

It was Daniel.

"Come with me," said Todd. "I do not wish to disturb Miss Bute's lesson any more. We will do what we must do outside. Continue your lesson, Miss Bute."

Tex and Daniel went to him, left the classroom with him. There was deep silence when the door was closed. Miss Bute continued to look at the closed door. There were tears in her eyes when she turned back to us.

"Robert," she said to me. "You must pair up with Dominic now."

❧ TWENTY-FIVE ❧

Daniel sat with us on the bus home that day.

"How many did you get?" said Col.

"Four," said Daniel. He showed us the dark marks crossing his palms. "Don't worry," he said. "I'll get him back."

"Oh, aye?" said Col.

"Yes," said Daniel. "He can't get away with going on like that."

"Oh, no?" said Col. "He's famous for it, man. Sacred Heart's hard man. He's always done it and he always will and there's nowt nobody can do."

"What if your dad sees?" said Diggy.

Daniel looked: What did Diggy mean?

"Sees what?" he said.

"The strap marks. If my dad saw I'd been belted, he'd give us another ploating hisself."

"But I didn't do anything, Diggy."

"That means nowt. He'd bliddy kill us, man."

"I bet Tex gets clouted," said Ed.

Daniel laughed and shook his head and sat back in his seat and looked at us all. I thought of his dad, with his jeans and leather jacket and his hair curling over his collar.

"Maybe my dad should come and photograph your dad," Daniel said to Diggy.

"You haven't seen the mush on him," said Diggy. "He'd break the bliddy camera. Me mother, now, she looks canny. But no. If anybody tried photographing her, they'd get ploated and all. Mebbes he'd better just keep out the way."

I got off with Daniel at the Rat. We walked down his lane together to the beach. I told him more about McNulty: the fire-breathing, the chains, the little sack for coins.

"Me dad knew him from the war," I said.

"And he's come back in time for the next war."

"D'you think so?"

"The Russians just exploded the biggest bomb the world's ever known. The explosion was six miles high. They say that they wondered if the explosion would ever stop, or if it would just keep on and on and never stop."

"It couldn't do that, could it?"

"My dad says they're playing with things they don't understand. They don't know the forces they might unleash."

We approached his house.

"Are you in a hurry?" he said. "D'you want to come inside or..."

He toed the sand.

I shrugged.

"Aye," I said. "OK."

There was no one in. He let himself in with his own key. There were boxes full of books in the hallway. He laughed.

"We're still getting sorted out," he said. "Look at them all. Books, books, books!"

He got some biscuits out of a tin and we ate them in the room with the big window facing the sea. Plaster had been ripped off the walls of the room so the stone showed through. There was a thick cream carpet. There was a white record player on a wide shelf and a load of records.

"We listen to music all the time," said Daniel. "Jazz, pop, that sort of stuff. Do you?"

I shook my head.

"Just the wireless sometimes," I said. I chewed my biscuit and watched a trawler on the sea. I wanted to say that my mam sang a lot but I didn't. I wanted to find some common ground but I couldn't.

"Do you play football or anything?" I said.

"I'm a runner. I won the sprint in my school sports day. I was given a small silver cup."

"Sometimes we play up past the tip. You could come and join in."

"Maybe I could."

"You must've had loads of mates down in Kent, eh?"

"Yeah. They said they'll come to see me, but it's not exactly near, is it?"

He went to a shelf and started turning over some pictures.

"Something to show you," he said.

He passed me a black-and-white photograph, a foot wide. It was our house, with a stretch of sand in front and the sky above with a few wispy clouds in it. Nothing else. It looked dead still. It looked ancient and new at the same time.

"See them?" he said. "Look closer."

As I looked more closely, I saw the three faces beyond the front window, hardly visible, hardly there at all.

"See yourselves?" he asked.

"Aye."

We were like three pale ghosts, half in and half out of the darkness.

"Have it," said Daniel. "Go on, he makes loads of prints of the ones he likes."

I looked again. I saw the twist in the door frame, the dip in the roof ridge, the thin cracks in the front wall. I saw the three faces again.

"Maybe it'll be one that gets into his book," he said.

I turned my eyes away. I breathed.

"What else is there?" I asked.

"Oh, lots of stuff." He flicked through the prints again. "This one's his favorite so far."

He turned it over. It was Ailsa and her family in the sea. They were dark curved figures, dark as the coal that was heaped on the cart behind them, dark as Wilberforce, who stared gloomily toward the land. Ailsa stretched down with her hands toward the water. Her dad held a great bucket on his shoulder. Losh and Yak strode through the breaking waves with their shovels.

"They look great, don't they?" said Daniel. "Dad says they look like ancient devils or something."

"What do you mean?"

"Like something from ancient tales. Half human. He says you'd only find them in a place like Keely Bay."

"You think we're all like that?"

He shrugged. He looked down, but I saw the grinning in his eyes.

I pointed.

"That's Ailsa," I said.

"That stubby round thing? Is that the one that should've come to school but didn't?"

"Aye."

"She must be stupid."

"Is that what you think?"

"Yes. She's a waster."

"And that's her dad, Mr. Spink. And that's her brothers, Losh and Yak. And that's Wilberforce."

"Wilberforce!"

"Aye. Wilberforce."

"Bloody hell."

I clenched my fists. I wanted to grab him and fight him there and then.

"Look at the state of them," he said. "How long have they been doing this?"

"Forever."

"Bloody hell. What a life."

I was going to hit him when I looked out and saw Joseph out on the beach, at the shoreline, looking toward us. Daniel saw him too.

"He's got him as well," he said. "The jeans and the boots and the oily hair and the cigarettes. Says you'd only get somebody like him in a place like this. Another throwback."

"He's Joseph Connor," I said. "He's my friend. He's worth ten of you."

"Do you think so?"

"Aye."

"That shows how stupid you are as well, doesn't it?"

I raised my hands.

"Are you going to fight me?" he mocked. "That's what you do up here, isn't it? Scrap and fight like animals."

He curled his lip. He raised his own hands, fists clenched.

"Come on, then," he said. "You think you can beat me easily, don't you? Come on, then. Prove it. You might be in for a surprise."

He laughed at me. I lowered my hands. I left the house. I went toward the sea. Joseph waited for me there. His face was cold.

"What you doing in there?" he said.

"Nowt."

"Nowt? Well, this is for nowt, then."

He grabbed me by the scruff of the neck, then shoved me down. I knew Daniel would be watching as I sprawled at the edge of the sea like a half-human thing while Joseph walked away.

❧ TWENTY-SIX ❧

When I got in, Dad was sitting there in the front room reading the *Chronicle*.

"What you doing in?" I said.

"Been to the doctor," he said.

"What for?"

"Nowt."

Mam came to the doorway.

"It's nothing, Bobby," she said. "He had a funny turn at work. But look at him. Fit as a lop."

There was a box of aspirin and the Gypsy's twist of paper and a half-empty bottle of Lourdes water on the sideboard.

"Flu or something," said Dad. "It's under attack from all quarters."

I showed them the photograph of the house and they laughed.

"Fancy taking a picture of our house," Mam said.

"It might be in a book," I told her.

"Fame at last," said Dad; then he caught his breath. "There's us, look, love."

Mam stared.

"Well, I never," she said. She laughed. "I should've done me hair."

"You cannot see nowt, man," he said. "You'd need a bloody magnifying glass to make us out. Done me hair! Look at that roof, eh? Looks like it could cave in any minute."

He coughed and swallowed. Mam looked at him, then looked away. He took a deep breath and laughed.

"Hey," he said. "Look what else I dug out of that cupboard, son."

He reached over the side of his chair and lifted a hat up. It was a high brown felt hat with a wide rim. He put it on his head. One side of the rim was horizontal, the other was vertical. He saluted.

"It's me Burma hat," he said. He coughed again and couldn't get his words out for a while. "Not seen it since you were a twinkle in me eye," he said at last.

He held it out to me.

"Smell it," he said.

I held it to my nose.

"Smell deep enough and you'll smell the jungle and the war and the journey home."

I breathed. I tried to imagine the smells of such

strange and distant things. I put the hat on my head and it fell down and hooded my eyes.

"Was hardly more than a bairn meself when I first put that on," he said.

He coughed again. He recovered himself. He put the hat back on his own head. Then he got up and marched toward the window.

"Ten-shun!" he snapped.

He stood dead still, a silhouette against the sea and sky.

"He's got to have a checkup at the hospital," whispered Mam. "But don't worry, Bobby. He's fine."

❧ TWENTY-SEVEN ❧

My homework was about skin, its elasticity, its networks of nerve endings, its blood vessels and sweat glands and follicles, its loops and whorls, its textures, its colors, the way it reacts to heat and cold, the way it reddens and whitens, the way it trembles and creeps, the way it keeps the outside out and the inside in, but how the barrier is broken time and again by germs and sweat and biting insects and how easy it is to pierce, how easy it is to draw blood. I wrote a couple of pages. I drew a few diagrams. Then I stopped. I got my blazer and searched the seams. I found Mam's tacking pin. I sat in front of the Lourdes light and started touching the needle point to my skin. In the places where I felt nothing, I pressed harder until I could feel something. In one or two places, I drew tiny bulbs of blood. I pushed the needle into the hard skin at the edge of my thumbnail and found I could push it all the way through and feel no

pain. I tried other places, but could tell that I'd quickly
be in agony. I closed my eyes and tried to imagine being
McNulty. I held an imaginary skewer and mimed pushing it from cheek to cheek. How could he do such a
thing? I went downstairs. Mam and Dad were watching
telly. I told them I was getting a drink of water. I found
a box of matches and took them upstairs. I opened my
window to let the smell out. I lit a match. I touched the
flame with my fingertip and gasped with pain. But I
found I could run my finger through the flame and feel
next to nothing. I practiced doing it slowly and more
slowly. I tried to imagine being McNulty. I held a
lighted match before my open mouth and drew it closer,
closer. I flinched from its heat. I imagined taking a great
blazing torch into my mouth. How could he do such a
thing? I went to the little bookshelf on the landing. I
found a picture of St. Sebastian with a dozen arrows in
him and his eyes turned toward heaven. I read about
saints who fasted and whipped themselves and went
mad and spent years in wild places. Why did they do
such things? What was the point of all that pain? I
thought of Jesus writhing on his cross. What did it
mean, that his pain had helped to save us? I went back
to my room and watched night falling over the sea.
The light turned, the sea turned, the stars came out. I
breathed the night air. I wanted to stop being me, just
for a moment, a second. I wanted to break free of my
skin, to be the sea, the sky, a stone, the lighthouse light,

to be out there in the gathering darkness, to be nothing, unconscious, wild and free.

"Bobby! Bobby!"

"Yes, Mam?"

"Howay, son. Leave them books. I've put some cocoa on."

❧ TWENTY-EIGHT ❧

Another Sunday morning. I went to the quayside again with Mam but McNulty was nowhere to be seen. We drank hot mugs of tea. We watched the seagulls plunging from their nests on the underside of the bridge. We inspected the rainbow patterns on the surface of the river. Mam bought some scarves for the coming winter and as she passed the money over, she said, "There's often a man here. He breathes fire and..."

The stall holder had a thick woollen coat on and thick gloves.

"Oh, him," she said. "The nutter. He's not been seen. Just as well, if you ask me. You call that entertainment? Should be strung up, if you ask me."

We took the lift up to the bridge again. The man inside remembered us. He giggled and showed us the entry in his notebook.

"See," he said. "You're written down. You really do exist."

He ushered us out.

"Goodbye, madam," he said. "Farewell, young sir." He dictated our new entry to himself. "The return visit from a lady and her son..."

We looked down from the bridge, but still no sign of McNulty. We walked back up into the city. We headed homeward in the bus. I looked out at the streets and then the fields and lanes, hoping that I'd see him. Mam hummed "Bobby Shafto" at my side.

At home, Dad was roaring with laughter as we went in.

"Come and see!" he said. "Quick! Come and see!"

He had the TV on. There was a man in a sports jacket smoking a pipe. A Labrador lay peacefully at his side. There was a deep hole in the ground. It had a concrete floor and it was lined with concrete blocks.

"It is important that the walls are at least ten inches thick," he said. "The roof, of course, should also be of concrete. And this roof should ideally be at least four feet underground."

He pointed downward with his pipe.

"This, then," he said, "is the basic construction of your family fallout shelter. The shelves are for storing food and water supplies. The cabinet here is for your chemical lavatory. A radio will be essential for keeping up to date with what's going on outside. Beyond the basics, though, let your invention run riot. TV sets, hi-fi systems . . . the possibilities are endless!"

He puffed on his pipe.

"We have estimated that it would take two men three weeks to build. Give or take a day or so, depending on fitness, strength, age, availability of materials, nature of the ground to be dug, weather conditions, et cetera, et cetera. Helpful leaflets with detailed plans are available. With good materials and proper construction, the shelter will be able to withstand an attack of several megatons." He smiled and stroked his dog. "Beyond this, we're in need of a lady's touch."

And a woman in a flowery dress walked on, smiling.

"Now then," she said. "Move aside, John. What can we do to make this more like home? And how are we going to occupy those kiddies for all that time? Well, here's a few suggestions, girls."

"Hell's teeth," said Dad.

"The world's gone mad," said Mam.

She clicked it off. We said nothing for a while.

"He wasn't there," said Mam eventually.

"Who?" said Dad.

"McNulty."

"That's a shame."

"Hope he's OK, eh?"

"Aye."

Dad looked at me.

"D'you think we count as two men?" he said. "A scrawny brat like you and an old wheezer like me?"

I shook my head.

"It'd take us more than three weeks, then, eh?"

"Aye," I said.

"We'd better get started this afternoon, then?"

"Better had."

"Have you got a shovel?"

I shook my head.

"Or some concrete?" he said.

I shook my head.

"Pity," he said. "Mebbes we'll leave it awhile, then."

"Aye," I said.

"Aye."

❧ TWENTY-NINE ❧

Later, I went to see Ailsa. Yak was in the yard, heaving coal from the cart to the pickup truck.

"Allreet, Bobby lad?" he called.

"Aye," I said.

"She's in the kitchen." He winked. "Nae lovey-dovey stuff, mind. She's got our tea to make. OK?"

I just looked at him.

"How's that new school ganning?" he said.

"Fine."

"You'll soon be too posh to gan on the cart, I s'pose?"

"No, I won't."

"That's allreet, then. But you'll be learning tons, eh?"

"Aye."

"Top of the class, are ye?"

"No, I'm not."

"Course ye are, kidder. I kna ye. Head stuffed full of

brains. So answer us this. What d'you call a bloke with nae lugs?"

"I don't know. What do you call a bloke with no lugs?"

"Do they teach you nowt in that place? You call him owt you like 'cos he cannot hear you."

I found Ailsa in the kitchen with an apron on. She was rolling pastry.

"Rabbit pie," she said. "Losh shot it. You could stay if you like." It smelt delicious. "Go on. Your mam wouldn't mind."

"Mebbe," I said. "Do you not get sick of it?"

"Of what?"

"Looking after them."

"No," she said. "I love them. And since me mam died..."

"How's the fawn?"

"Grand. Getting stronger."

She took a bowl out of the oven. A dark bubbling stew. She laid the pastry over the top of it. She trimmed the edges. She quickly made the shape of a rabbit from spare pastry and put it at the center. Then she put the whole thing back in the oven and rubbed the flour from her hands. I thought of what Mam said: It isn't right. The girl's too young for such a life. What can her dad be thinking of?

"Isn't it weird?" she said. "I cook the rabbit but I look after the fawn. Do you understand it?"

"Not really."

"Me neither, and they'll not teach you that at school. They come again, you know."

"Who did?"

"The buggers from the council. They were in a big black car. 'We've come to get your daughter to go to school,' they said. 'Have you now?' says Dad. 'You and whose army?' says Yak. 'We don't want any trouble now,' they says, 'and we know you folk is independent-minded, but it's the law, Mr. Spink.' One of them turns to us, a big fat feller with specs and goggly eyes. 'Do you not want to pursue your education, little lady?' he says. 'No,' I say. 'You'll be left behind, you know,' he says. 'This is a time of opportunities and great improvement for common folk like you. All the other bairns is grabbing their opportunities.' 'I diven't care,' I says. 'I'm happy.' 'See?' says Yak. 'But it's the law, Mr. Spink,' says Goggle Eyes. 'Then you can take your law,' says Losh, 'and stick it up your hairy arse. Now hadaway. We've got work to do.'"

"And did they go?" I said.

"Oh, aye, but they'll be back. They said the police might have to get involved. 'Then so might this shovel of mine,' says Losh. They scarpered back to the car and off they went."

She peeled a potato, cutting away a perfect curling slice of skin.

"They'll be back," she said. "And probably I'll end up

going. But it's fun to keep them hopping, like me daddy says. Boring buggers."

I helped her to peel the potatoes. She put them on to boil. We set the table. "Aye," I said, when she asked again if I would stay for tea. "Me mam'll know I'm here."

We drank some of her lemonade.

"Ailsa," I said. "What was it like when your mother died?"

She rolled her eyes.

"Oh, it was just great!" She laughed. "It was such fun! What do you think it was like? It was horrible. It was the worst thing. It was..."

She looked at me.

"What's wrong?" she said.

"Nowt."

Then her dad and her brothers came in, filthy and huge and with their eyes sparkling in filthy faces.

"We're feeding Hollow Legs, are we?" said Yak. "You should've shot a cow, Losh."

They washed their hands in a basin by the door, lit cigarettes and swigged big glasses of beer.

Ailsa's dad put his arms around me and Ailsa.

"These lovely bairns," he said. "They're a credit to each and every one of us."

✵ THIRTY ✵

Later Ailsa and I went out and we stood in the sea beneath the stars.

"Every one's a million million miles away," I said. "And they look tiny, but every one of them's a massive sun."

A shooting star streaked through the sky and for an instant was the brightest thing above.

"And that's mebbe no bigger than a fingernail," I said.

I kicked the water with my bare feet. The lighthouse light swept across us.

"Why's it all so bloody hard?" I said.

She laughed.

" 'Cos you think too much," she said.

I knew she was right. I tried to empty my mind of everything but the sea, the night and Ailsa.

"What did you do to heal the fawn?" I said.

"I told you."

"Was it really that easy?"

"Lemon squeezy."

"Will you do it for me dad?"

"Your dad?"

"I think he's really ill. Will you tell God to make him better?"

"Course I will. But you do it and all. Two folk asking's got a better chance than one. What's wrong with him?"

"I dunno. It's probably nowt."

"It'll be a piece of cake, then."

She laughed at me again.

"You're a strange'n, Bobby Burns. Let's do it now."

"Eh?"

"Let's do the asking now. Howay."

She led me to the water's edge. We knelt on the wet sand. She put her hands together.

"Howay," she said, so I put my hands together too.

"Close your eyes," she said, so I closed my eyes.

"Make Bobby's dad better," she said. "Say it, Bobby."

"Make Dad better," I said.

I peeped into the endless sky.

"Say it again," she said. "Will it to happen. Speak to God."

"Make Dad better," I whispered.

"Now wish and wish and wish and wish," she said.

I felt the water seeping through the sand. I felt the cold breeze from the sea. I saw the brightness of the lighthouse light sweep across my closed eyelids. I tried to wish and wish and pray and pray. I tried to imagine God looking down at us from somewhere past the stars. What would he look like? And why would he look down on this place, this coaly beach by a coaly sea, when there was all the universe to look at? Why would he hear us, a pair of kids? Why should he listen to us?

"What if there is no God?" I said.

"Mebbe that doesn't matter. And mebbe it doesn't matter to God if you think he's there or not. And wondering about them things certainly isn't going to help your dad, is it?"

"No."

"So put the wondering out of your mind and say it and wish it and do it properly as you can."

I closed my eyes and wished and prayed.

"That's better," she said. "It'll take a lot of doing. That little fawn was just a little fawn. It's probably harder to get it to work for a grown man."

We prayed again. I opened my eyes and saw her eyes shining brightly as she laughed at me.

"So let's hope it's nowt after all, eh, Bobby Burns?"

"Yes," I said, and already I felt happier.

"Your dad's strong as a cart horse," she said.

Then she peered past me.

"Who the hell's this?" she said.

❧ THIRTY-ONE ❧

A dark hunched figure, the shape of a man. A shadow, a moving silhouette. It moved toward us from the south, through the night, skimming the water's edge. It moved quickly, legs striding forward. A sack bounced at its back. It kept its head down. No eyes glittered. We knelt there and didn't move and hardly breathed. Ailsa pressed against my side. It was a man, in heavy boots, with a dark cap pulled tight on his head, with a dark jacket buttoned tight. We heard the water splashing beneath his feet. As he approached, we heard the rasping of his breath. I smelt fire, smoke, paraffin. And then the lighthouse light came round again.

"McNulty!" I gasped.

He didn't pause. He didn't see us. He splashed straight past us. I held my hand up.

"McNulty!"

He didn't turn. He continued northward toward the

lighthouse headland, the rock pools, the dunes, the pines.

"McNulty?" said Ailsa.

"He's a fire-eater. An escapologist."

"I smelt him," she said.

I nodded.

"He's harmless," I said. "I saw him at the quay. He does things for money. My dad knew him, long ago in the war."

We stood up and watched him moving north. Soon he blended with the night. When the lighthouse light came round again there was no sign of him.

"What brings him here?" said Ailsa.

"He told me he might come."

"He told you? So why didn't he remember you?"

I shook my head. He had seemed so close, those days he stared into my eyes and held me and begged me for my help.

"His mind's gone," I said. "He doesn't remember things. He says he's like a little child."

We looked northward. We held our arms against the lighthouse light. It passed. Another star fell toward the sea.

"I'll tell you what it was like when she died," she said. "It was like the whole world was the devil's place. Like there'd never be any goodness, ever again. Like there'd never be any light."

She kissed my cheek.

"I love you, Bobby Burns," she said.

I felt my face burning.

"Say it, Bobby," she said. "Say you love me too."

"I love you, Ailsa Spink."

And then we ran: from each other, from the shining stars, from the turning sea, from the yawning spaces of the night, from the presence or the absence of God, from the devil McNulty, from the aching in our hearts that threatened to overwhelm us.

"Good night, Bobby," she yelled.

"Good night, Ailsa. Good night!"

❧ THIRTY-TWO ❧

I started to tell Mam about it when I got in.

"I saw—" I said.

She put her finger to her lips.

"Quieter, Bobby," she said. She pointed upstairs. "He's having a sleep, and he needs his sleep. It's hospital tomorrow."

"I saw McNulty on the beach," I whispered.

"Did you now?"

"He was heading north."

"Was he now?"

She tilted her head and listened. We heard Dad groaning, snoring.

"McNulty?" she whispered.

"It was dark, I couldn't see him properly, but it was him."

She absentmindedly stroked my shoulder.

"Mebbe you just imagined it, Bobby," she murmured.

"Mebbe. What's wrong with him, Mam?"

"Nothing, son. We'll find out. He'll be right as rain."

We listened. Just deep silence, and the never-ending rumble of the sea.

❧ THIRTY-THREE ❧

The biology room again. We sat around a table, all of us, gathered around Miss Bute. She had a tall glass jar between her hands. Ghostly beasts dangled there, heads and limbs and tails distorted by the curves of the glass, by the liquid that contained them.

"This time you must behave," she said.

We nodded.

"Yes, miss," we said. "Dead right, miss."

We breathed at the memory of Todd. We glanced at the closed doors.

"It's not only because of that," she said.

She began to unscrew the lid of the jar.

"It's also because these were once living things. And like all living things, they were sacred."

She took off the lid and the weird scent of formaldehyde rose to us. Some of us put our hands across our noses and mouths. Some of us caught our breath in apprehension. She put down the lid, lifted a pair of tongs.

"Once they were as alive as you are," she said. "Remember that."

She dipped the tongs into the jar. She peered down and gently moved the beasts. Then caught a head between the tongs and lifted a creature from the liquid. She held it over the jar for a few seconds, letting the liquid drain from it. Then laid it on a clean white cloth. It was a frog. She lifted it again and held it in her palm, showed us the powerful long back legs, the short forelegs. She showed us the webbed feet, the smooth slick skin.

"See how perfectly it was made," she said, "how perfectly it was suited for its life between air and water."

She stroked its cheek. It gazed at her through dead, clouded, empty eyes.

"Pretty thing," she murmured.

She laid it down again, on its back. She gently tugged its legs until it was splayed on the cloth.

"Does it look strange?" she asked us. "Eerie? Alien? Very different to us?"

"Yes, miss," someone murmured.

"Never seen one up so close," said another.

"The Thing from Planet Zog," said another.

"And yet it's also familiar," said Miss Bute. "It shares our world and we know it and recognize it. It is our neighbor. A frog. Perfect in its frogginess."

She sighed as she lifted a scalpel. She looked to Jesus, hanging there in agony above the door.

"This is for the best of purposes," she said.

She turned her eyes back to us.

"The word for this is *dissection*," she said. "The cutting apart of the dead. It is never to be undertaken lightly."

We gasped as she started to cut. She cut the frog vertically from throat to groin. Then made another cut, horizontal. With great tenderness, using her fingers and the scalpel tip, she teased back the flesh from her cross-shaped incision, she tugged open the tiny rib cage, she eased apart a pair of tiny lungs, and finally exposed the tiny heart.

"See," she whispered. "Skin, muscle, bone, lungs, heart. So alien and eerie and so just like us."

She stroked its cheek again.

"Forgive me, little frog," she said.

She put the scalpel down.

"At least she is beyond pain," she said.

Next she reached to a shelf behind her and brought down a battery with two thin wires wrapped around it. She put it down beside the frog, unwrapped the wires.

"What is missing?" said Miss Bute.

"Sorry, miss?"

"From the frog. What has it lost?"

"Its life, miss."

"Yes, its life. And if it had its life again?"

127

"Sorry, miss?"

"If it had its life again, what then?"

"It would feel pain again, miss."

"It'd hop off the table, miss."

"Its heart would beat again, miss."

"Ah," she said. "Its heart would beat again."

She took one of the thin wires and pressed it into the flesh on one side of its heart. She took the other wire and pressed it at the other side. She gently moved the two wires, seeking their proper place, and then we gasped again. Someone squealed. For the heart flickered. It flickered again. We crowded close. Miss Bute touched and touched again with the wire and the heart moved in rhythm. It beat, as it had when the frog was alive. She touched other parts of the frog and the legs twitched, the head twitched.

"So is the frog alive again?" she said.

"No, miss."

"Course not, miss."

"It's just a trick, miss."

She smiled.

"Yes. It's just a trick. A Frankensteiny trick."

She put the battery back. She eased back the frog's bones, flesh and skin. She pressed it tenderly with her palm. She looked at us.

"I'll ask the same question again. What is missing? What has the frog lost?"

"Life," someone said.

"So what is life?" she said.

We couldn't answer.

"Does a frog have a soul?" asked Mary Marr.

"Ask that question to a priest," said Miss Bute. "But what it does have is a mystery. We open it up to find an answer and the mystery only deepens. What is missing? What has been lost? What is life?"

Far off down a corridor, the bell rang.

"No homework," said Miss Bute. "Just remember what you've seen."

We filed out. Todd was outside the room, strap in hand. But we were quiet and subdued. He slid the strap back into his breast pocket. As we walked past him, Daniel murmured something.

"What was that, boy?" said Todd.

"Nothing, sir," said Daniel.

Todd narrowed his eyes. Daniel walked on, close behind me. Out of earshot, he murmured again.

"Smile, please."

I turned to look at him.

"I'll get our evil Mr. Todd," he said.

He winked.

"Smile, please, Mr. Todd, sir."

❦ THIRTY-FOUR ❦

"Psst! Psst!"

When I got off the bus that evening, Joseph was waiting for me.

"Psst! Bobby!"

He was in the hawthorn. I remembered how he'd shoved me down in the sand. How many times could I let him get away with it? I tried to walk by without acknowledging him, but he came out to me. He held my elbow.

"Bobby, man."

I looked at him. He lowered his eyes.

"I know," he said. "I shouldn't've done it." He shrugged. "I didn't mean nowt, man. I just get carried away. You know that, man."

"Do I?"

"Aye." He gritted his teeth. "I'm just a stupid plonker, man. I'm sorry. OK?"

I shook my head. I knew I was about to let him get away with it again.

"How sorry?" I said.

"Dead sorry."

"Dead dead sorry?"

"Aye."

"Say it."

"I'm dead dead sorry."

"Bobby."

"Eh?"

"Say, I'm dead dead sorry, Bobby."

"I'm dead dead sorry, Bobby."

"Sir."

"Eh?"

"Say, I'm dead dead sorry, Bobby, sir."

He grinned. We looked at each other.

"Hadaway and shite," he said.

"Aye," I said. "OK."

He rubbed his hands.

"Right," he said. "That's done. I want you to come with me. Something to show you."

"What is it?"

"Another incomer. A weird one."

I knew that it must be McNulty.

"Where is he?" I said.

"I'll show you. Howay."

We headed toward the beach, close together, shoulders bumping each other as we walked. He hung about as I went into the house to drop my bag off and get changed. Mam and Dad were in the kitchen. Dad was on a stool with a cup of tea in his hand.

"You OK, then?" I said.

"Right as rain," he said. "They took half an armful of blood. They looked deep into me lovely eyes, then deep into me throat. They stuck a torch in me lugs and a tube up me bum. And how many X-rays was it, love?"

Mam shoved a buttered scone into my hand.

"Seven," she said. "Or was it eight?"

"So if there's owt to find, they'll find it, then they'll fix it. But there'll be nowt to find."

I looked at them. They both looked away.

"I'm going out for a bit," I said. "With Joseph."

She clicked her tongue and shook her head, but she got another scone.

"Go on," she said. "One for him and all, I suppose."

I let her kiss me.

"Tea'll be on the table in an hour," she said. "No later."

I hurried out.

"She's a bliddy great cook," Joseph said as he led me toward the lighthouse and the pines. "Remember them times I used to come for dinner?"

"Aye."

"Them steak pies, man!"

He smacked his lips at the memory. We chewed the scones. We walked across the sand toward the lighthouse headland. The tide was far out. There was a long line of jetsam left behind: heaps of seaweed, timber carved to smooth strange shapes, bits of net, fishermen's ropes, broken fish boxes, seashells, crab shells, desiccated starfish, bottles, a tire, a dead gannet, stones, pebbles, glinting glass. I reached down and picked up a leather shoe. It seemed something ancient, was stiff as a board, but with its pointed toe and its thin sole had probably been lost or thrown away just a few weeks ago. I slung it back toward the sea. I lifted a bone. It was dried and bleached and worn, but it was a mammal's bone, maybe a thighbone. I let myself imagine it was a bone from one of Ailsa's drowned sailors, then threw it also toward the sea. Joseph smoked and the scent of it mingled with the seaweed stench, the salt, the airy autumn smell of the sea. I threw stones, and watched the way they spun and curved and twisted in the air.

Then we crossed the stony headland and entered the pines.

"I know who you've found," I said.

"You know him?"

"He's called McNulty. I told you about him. The strongman, the escapologist, the..."

"Him?"

"Aye."

"So what's he doing here?"

"Dunno."

Ahead of us were dunes, with the ancient holiday

shacks in them. Some of them were breaking up, sinking into the sand. Others were better preserved, with fresh paint, felted roofs, little fenced-off gardens. Their doors were locked and there were boards at the windows for protection against the coming winter. They were places that had been built by pitmen generations back, places for holidays beside the coaly sea. Several had names carved into their front doors: Buckingham Hut, Desandoris, Dunhewing, Worgate Manor. I knew that Daniel's dad had been among them with his camera, that they'd look like things of wonder in his book.

"Look," said Joseph.

Smoke was rising, a narrow plume of it. We headed toward it. As we waded through the soft sand and the knee-high marram grass, I told Joseph what I knew about McNulty: the war, Burma, escapology, fire-eating.

"Fire-eating?" he said. "Always wanted to have a go at that."

He struck a match and quickly pushed the flame into and out of his wide-open mouth. Then he lit a cigarette that crackled as he drew on it. He sucked the smoke deep down.

"Aaaaaah," he said as the smoke seethed out again. "Lovely."

Then he pondered.

"Mind you," he said, "if he's really cracked we'll mebbe have to drive him out."

"Drive him out?"

"There's bairns round here, Bobby. There's no telling what a bloke like him might do."

"He's harmless."

"That's what they always say. We'll see."

We stooped as we got closer to the smoke. We climbed a hill of sand. We peered through the grass into a depression in the earth. There was McNulty, outside a half-ruined green-painted shack. He knelt in front of his little fire, feeding it sticks, and it glowed more strongly in the fading light. He drank from a little bottle. He nibbled at some bread. He crouched with his head on his knees and bobbed back and forward as if praying. He held his hands palm upward toward the sky. Then he sat cross-legged, eyes closed, dead still. The grass around him shifted gently in the breeze. High above, a single seagull screamed. The light continued fading. Then McNulty leaned forward and lowered his hands into the fire and let them rest there for a moment. Joseph gasped. Then McNulty lit a torch and breathed flames into the air, then seemed to breathe them in again, right into himself. "Beautiful," whispered Joseph. Then McNulty turned and looked toward us. We slithered backward. But right away, McNulty was above us, standing there against the sky.

"You got to pay," he said. "You got to pay!"

I stared full into his face, willing him to see me and know me. "Mr. McNulty," I said, but Joseph dragged me away, and we ran, slipping and tumbling through the sand. At the pines we stood gasping and giggling. Our hearts thundered. McNulty hadn't followed us. He was nowhere to be seen.

"Lock your doors!" yelled Joseph.

Then we hurried onward, and the sky above our heads was a storm of screaming gulls and the sea was roaring in again.

❧ THIRTY-FIVE ❧

I shoved meat and gravy into my mouth. The curtains were shut. The fire blazed at my back.

"Good time?" said Dad.

"Aye," I said.

"Where'd you go?"

I shrugged and raised my hands: just out. I knew he wouldn't pry.

"Good lad. I see the dark's in your eyes tonight."

He smiled.

"They're the best times, eh? Out with your mates in darkening nights. Winter coming on, chilly air, thumping heart." He swigged his glass of beer. "They say that summer's best and mebbe it is in the long run, but there's nowt to beat the fun of summer's end and the turn to autumn. All that sense that things is doomed and all that gathering scariness."

He laughed at himself.

"Listen to Mister Romantic," said Mam. "What he means is there's nowt to beat a nice warm meal in a nice warm chair by a nice warm fire."

She reached out and rubbed his stomach, then spooned vegetables onto his plate.

"Come on," she said. "Eat up, man. You need your strength."

"One time," he said, and his eyes glittered as they turned toward the past, "one November, me and Ted Garbutt slept out all night in the dunes. Just a blanket and a slice of tarpaulin for each of us and a hunk of bread and a bottle of cold tea and the fire crackling and the ghostly tales we told each other. Hell, the ghouls and monsters we magicked with our words to roam the beach that night. They crept in the shadows of the dunes and whispered in the hissing of the flames and reached into our blankets with their claws and bony fingers. I can hear Ted still: There's a goblin in the fire! The way we screamed! And who knew where the laughter finished and the terror started?"

Mam rolled her eyes at me. She winked.

"He's in his dotage, son. It was all a long long time ago."

He swigged his beer.

"Aye, it was. I'm glad we did them things, had times like that. There was hardship enough all around us but what did we care? We were bairns, free and easy. Who were we to know the war'd be so soon upon us?"

He coughed and retched, and held his hand to his chest, and tears flooded his eyes. He blinked.

"So you make sure you get your good times in, son. You never know what's round the corner."

Later, he nodded off in his armchair. Mam and I looked at each other, said nothing. Then she opened the handbag she always kept by the side of her chair.

"You ever seen this one?" she said.

It was a photograph of her when she was young. It was so tiny. She laid it at the center of my palm. Just her face, the collar of a pale blouse, and a narrow border of white around her. It had darkened. It seemed as though it could have come from centuries ago.

"The fading's because of the heat," she said. "He took it with him to Burma. He carried it in his tunic pocket against his heart. Mister Softie. He said it went with him always and everywhere."

She smiled and stroked my hair.

"He said it was his lucky charm and it kept him alive. He said he knew that if he carried it with him he'd come home to me again."

She looked up at me from the photograph, young and lovely, laughing eyes. I felt her breath on me.

"Do you know how privileged you are?" she said.

"Privileged?"

"Aye. It's not a word that many'd think of when they think of us. Privileged. To have a dad like him and be from a place like this and..."

She smiled.

"Aye," I said. "I know."

She took the photo from me, then leaned toward Dad. She kissed his cheek, then slipped the photograph into the breast pocket of his shirt.

"Look after him again," she said.

I was going to tell her about McNulty then, but there were tears in her eyes and it didn't seem the right time. I went up to my room. I did my homework of remembering; then I gazed into the night and watched the moonlit breakers crashing on the shore. When I slept, I dreamed that McNulty crept through the dunes and entered the house and came upstairs to lie in bed with Dad. They whispered together about Burma; then the bed became a boat and they clutched each other tight as they rocked and reeled in the stormy sea that carried them toward another war.

❊ THIRTY-SIX ❊

The first photograph of Todd appeared next morning. It was pinned to the notice board just inside the school's front door. It had been taken in the schoolyard. There were lots of kids in it, standing about in groups, playing football, lost in thought. Todd, in this one, was just a figure in the crowd. He held the pose that had quickly become so familiar to all of us. One hand was stretched out to hold a kid's forearm still; his other hand was raised, about to strike downward with the strap. The kid was Martin Keane, a second-year.

"Aye, that was me," I heard Martin say. "I took this shot and it hit the window. He give us two. He done the second right across me wrist, the sod." He puffed his chest out as he started to tell the tale again. "Aye, you're right, it's me...."

The photo was soon removed but not before a few dozen of us had seen it. We thought little more of it.

Then the second photograph appeared that afternoon. It was taped up in the science block toilets. It was the same photograph, but this time it was enlarged, so that Todd and Martin filled more of it. You could see the cold look on Todd's face, and the way Martin was flinching. Loads of lads saw it, and even the girls started coming in. One of the science teachers, Bunsen Brooks, took this one down. I was there when he came in. He clicked his tongue, as if it was all just a little thing.

"Come on," he said. "The show's over. What's all the fuss?"

He yanked it off the wall, but underneath there was black ink, the single word, EVIL. Bunsen ran his fingers across it.

"Who knows anything about *this?*" he said.

We looked back at him. Nobody.

On the bus home that day, Diggy said, "Wouldn't like to be in his shoes when they find him."

"Todd'll kill him," said Col.

"Aye," said Ed. "I wonder who it is."

I looked at Daniel. He lounged with his knees up, reading. He met my eye for a second. He lowered his eyes again. As he began to read again, he let a finger cross his lips: *Keep quiet.*

"Was it you?" I said as we stepped down outside the Rat.

"You don't want to know too much," he said. "Keep mum. First rule in resistance. Anyway, whoever it is, it's a bit different, eh? Stops things getting yawn yawn yawn."

He pulled his collar close against the wind, looked up into the bleak gray sky.

"Hell's teeth," he said. "This is it, then? Northern winter on its way."

He pressed his finger to his lips and headed away.

Next day it was different. This time the image was much closer in: just Todd and Martin right in the foreground, the strap at the top edge of the photograph, Martin's hand at the bottom. You saw the true fear in Martin's eyes, the true cold contempt in Todd's. As we were looking at this one, which was pasted over a photograph of last year's school athletic team, there was news of several more. They'd been found throughout the school: on walls, dropped into desks, slipped into library books. There were several new images now, all of them containing Todd and his strap. Sometimes words accompanied them, written on the walls beneath or scrawled across the photographs themselves. Simple words: EVIL, WICKED, CRUELTY, SIN. The photographs quickly became collectors' items. Those that weren't taken down by staff were hidden deep in satchels and workbags. The most famous image was of Todd and the Whitby twins, Julia and John. The twins had their hands out together, side by side. They leaned their heads together and closed their eyes as the black strap descended.

In the classroom, Lubbock prowled through the aisles between our desks. His breath seethed.

"I pray that there is no one in this room connected to this business," he said. "There is a sly sneak at work. A serpent, a snake." He cracked his knuckles. "We will draw him out. He will slither out into the light. And then..." He licked his lips and sighed. There was silence as we worked, drawing a map of Jesus' journeys through the Holy Land. Then a crash as Lubbock smashed his fist onto Dorothy Peacock's desk. We jumped. We stared at him, his bulging flushed face.

"Mr. Todd," he snarled, "is worth ten of any of you inside this place."

He swept his hand across Dorothy's work. Her book and pencils flew onto the floor.

"Well!" he yelled. "What's the matter with you, girl? Pick them up! Pick them up!"

Dorothy scuttled to pick them up. Daniel raised his hand. He was expressionless.

"Sir!" he called.

Lubbock watched him, said nothing.

"Please, sir," said Daniel. "Could you show us where it was that Jesus gave the Sermon on the Mount?"

❧ THIRTY-SEVEN ❧

That afternoon, a special assembly was called. The whole school was ushered by prefects and grim-faced teachers through silent corridors toward the hall. The teachers mounted the stage and sat on hard chairs facing us. Many of them had their black gowns on. Todd was in the front row. His head was tilted, his eyes were lowered, his chest kept rising as he sighed, as if he'd been deeply wronged, as if he was in pain. His strap was nowhere to be seen.

Grace, the head, stepped forward. He carried a clutch of the photographs in his hand. He stared down at us for seconds; then he slowly started to rip the photographs. He bent forward and let the pieces fall into a waste bin at his feet.

"These objects," he said, "are worthy only of our contempt."

He wiped his hands together, as if cleaning away filth.

"We are a community," he continued. "It is our duty to care for each other, to protect each other, to ensure that none of us is made a victim of evil forces. When one of us is threatened, all of us are under threat."

He scanned our faces.

"There is a wicked force at work inside our school," he said. "We must not allow it to flourish. We must not allow it to corrupt us. The perpetrator—or perpetrators—of this evil may be standing beside you. Some of you will know who the perpetrators are. If you carry that knowledge, we call on you to speak up. Do not be intimidated. Your information will be received in confidence. At least one among you is that perpetrator. From you, whoever you are, we await a confession."

He was silent again. He searched our eyes. The teachers watched us. I felt my face burning. I looked downward.

"There is no hiding place," said Grace. "If shame will not drive you to us, then we shall search you out, just as the Lord searched out Adam and Eve in the Garden. Now, let us guide the sinner that is among us. We will recite the Confiteor."

And our voices joined together, began to groan the familiar prayer:

"I confess to Almighty God, to Blessed Mary ever virgin..." Soon each of us made a fist. We beat our hearts, as we'd learned to long ago, at the crucial words: "Through my fault, through my fault, through my most grievous fault."

Afterward, we were left standing for an hour. Grace walked among us. He barked at anyone who moved. He said that he would make our lives a hell. It made no difference. That night, I walked over the sand through the darkness to Daniel's place. I crouched in the garden, looked through the window. Daniel was with his parents. There were heaps of photographs on the table. They shook their heads as they looked at them. They clenched their fists, they glared. They drank wine and listened to jazz as they scrawled across the photographs and raised their fists and laughed together.

❧ THIRTY-EIGHT ☙

"**H**e's here, in the dunes," I said to Mam.

"Who is?"

"McNulty."

It was late in the evening. Dad had gone to bed early. She was stitching the seam of my new white shirt. We listened to the wind outside gathering force, rattling the roof, the window frames, the doors. We heard the waves crashing on the shore.

"He came a few nights back," I said. "He's in one of the old shacks."

"Maybe he wants to winter there. Keep himself safe and warm."

"We could take things to him. Bread or something. Tea."

Her voice rose and quickened.

"I can't care for two of them, Bobby," she said; then

she passed her hand across her eyes. "I'm sorry," she said. "Of course you can take him something."

She stitched on. Her needle slipped and pricked her finger.

"Damn thing!" she said. She flung the shirt aside. "Why can't they make things to last these days?"

She looked at her tiny wound. She sucked the blood from it.

"Sorry," she whispered. She looked away. "He's got to have some more tests, Bobby." She pressed her finger to her lips as I began to speak. "That's all we know. Nothing more."

We switched the TV on, but within seconds a mushroom cloud appeared.

"Not that!" she snapped, and she switched it off again.

That night I woke and heard him groaning. The winds had calmed. I knelt at the window, listened to the far-off drone of engines. He groaned again.

"Stop it," I whispered. "Let me be ill, not him."

I pressed my needle through the edge of my thumb. I pressed it into the flesh between my thumb and fore-finger.

"Let me take the pain," I said. "Not him."

I caught my breath and tears came to my eyes as I pressed the needle deeper.

"I can take it," I whispered.

He groaned again.

"Stop it! Leave him alone!"

I said a string of prayers: Hail Marys, Our Fathers, Confiteors. I touched Mary and Bernadette in their plastic grotto. Then I touched Ailsa's broken heart, McNulty's silver coin, the tanners from Ailsa's dad, the penknife from Joseph, the CND symbol.

"Leave him alone," I said again. "Take me instead of him."

I saw a star fall fast toward the sea. I searched my head for the words to make a wish. I found a promise.

"If he gets better," I said, "I'll always be good. I'll always fight evil."

That morning, I left home early. I waited for Daniel in the hawthorn hedge in his lane. At last he came.

"Psst!" I called. "Daniel!"

He looked in at me.

"I want to help you," I said.

"Help me?"

"With the photographs. I'll help you to put them out."

He came toward me.

"They'll catch us," he said. "You know that, don't you? I've always known, right from the start. Catching me's been part of it. They'll catch me in the act, or somebody will turn me in. It'll happen very soon. And when they catch me, then they'll have to face up to what the photographs show."

We gazed at each other.

"So they'll catch us," I said. I pulled my blazer open and showed him the CND symbol I'd pinned beside my heart. He grinned. "And we'll stand together," I said. "Side by side."

He opened his schoolbag. He showed me the photographs. Now they contained only Todd. His enlarged face filled each frame—teeth bared, froth at the corners of his mouth, eyes glaring down at some unseen victim—along with the repeated words: EVIL, WICKED, CRUELTY, SIN.

I nodded.

"They're great," I said.

We shook hands, he told me what to do, and that day I dropped his photographs into desks and dustbins and I slid them into library books. My only close shave was at lunchtime, when I scuttled out of the boys' changing room, where I'd left one in the showers. Miss Bute was passing by. She hesitated.

"Hello, Robert," she said.

"Miss."

"Is there sports club today?" she asked.

"Yes, miss. No, miss." I looked down. I felt so stupid, caught so soon. "I don't know, miss."

We stood there. For a moment I thought of opening my bag, showing her: *Yes, it's me, miss.*

She reached up and caught something in the empty air.

"Oh, look!" she said. "Hello, little dangler."

A tiny spider. It crawled across her palm, then hung from her finger on a string.

"Look at the skill of it," she said. "Look at its perfect spiderness."

She turned it three times around my head.

"It will bring you luck, Bobby. Make a wish."

I smiled.

"Thanks, miss."

She let the spider climb right down to earth; then she turned away.

"Take care of yourself, Bobby," she said.

❦ THIRTY-NINE ❦

Maybe Ailsa read my mind. It was late afternoon. I was doing my homework, a drawing of the skull, the way the bones are fused in it, the way the openings are formed in it, the way it's so beautifully made to protect the brain. I was shading in the pitch-black eye sockets. But my thoughts were in the dunes, seeking McNulty. I was about to ask Mam if I could take some food to him. There was a knocking at the door.

"Who's there?" called Mam.

"Ailsa Spink!" came the reply.

"Come in, pet!" yelled Mam.

Ailsa clicked the latch and stepped inside and stood there grinning.

"Hello, pet," said Mam, ruffling Ailsa's hair.

"I brought you these," said Ailsa. She opened a cloth and showed a plateful of jam tarts, all bright and glistening. "We had some spare, Mrs. Burns."

"Spare? Even with them ravenous men of yours?"

Ailsa winked.

"Kept them out of sight, sneaked them out the house. They'd eat the plates if I let them. Go on." She held them out to Dad. "I know you like them, Mr. Burns. Black currant or plum. They're lovely."

Dad smacked his lips and chose black currant. He ate. She held out the plate to Mam and me. We ate and grinned and licked the crumbs from our fingers and said how tasty they were.

"You'll have come for our Bobby, then?" said Dad.

"Distracting him from his work," said Mam. "Leading the poor lad astray."

Ailsa shrugged and pondered.

"That's right," she said.

Mam clicked her tongue.

"We hear you're still not going in," she said.

"I'm not," said Ailsa.

Mam pointed and wagged her finger.

"You'll regret it, you know. Silly lass. School could open up a whole new world for you."

Ailsa sighed. She stared at the ceiling.

"I know," she said. "And probably I will go in the end. Even stupid Losh and Yak know that. Then they'll lose their skivvy, eh?"

"Too much fire in you, that's your problem," said Dad. "You'll lead them a dance when you do go in." He grinned. "You'll be the brightest of them all."

We smiled together. I looked at Mam.

"Aye, go on," she said. "Long as you're back in time to finish it all."

I went upstairs and changed out of my uniform, then left the house with Ailsa. She lifted a package from the garden.

"More tarts," she said. "A bottle of warm tea. Howay."

"For McNulty," I said.

"That's right."

"I should take him something too."

I opened Dad's garden shed and took out two candles and some matches.

We walked quickly toward the dunes.

"We saw him wandering in the dunes," she said. "Me and Daddy and Losh and Yak. Losh thought he was some villain after the chickens or something; then we saw he was just like a poor lost soul. Running back and forward across the sand and his eyes all wild and he's jabbering to himself. He seen us and he tailed it. We followed him to his shack. I tell Daddy and the lads what you told me: the war, the quayside, the fire and the skewer. McNulty turned and looked before he went in. Stared at us like he's looking back across a thousand miles. Then he looks straight at me and points at me and goes, 'Come and help us, bonny bairn.' Losh stands right in front of me. He says nobody looks at his sister like that, and he's all for going straight down and kicking him on his way. But

Daddy says, 'Mebbe he's harmless, mebbe he'll go off of his own accord. Mebbe it could happen to any of us. Mebbe things has happened to him that'd drive any of us mad.' Losh grunts and spits. McNulty scuttles into the shack. We watch and wait. Nowt else happens. We head back to the house. I put the kettle on. Dad says I got to keep out of the dunes from now on. Losh and Yak's looking at each other. They're saying the wild man better keep away. Soon Yak's got a great big knife out and he's sharpening it on a stone."

We hurried through the pines.

"They'll drive him out," she said. "If it's not Losh and Yak it'll be somebody. We got to help him while we can."

We climbed the hill of sand.

❧ FORTY ❧

The sun was low over the moors to the west. It cast shadows into the hollow where McNulty's shack was. His fire smoldered outside. We watched and waited, but saw nothing. We walked down. The only window was broken and an ancient tattered curtain hung inside. The timbers were bleached as dry and pale as bone. The twisted door dangled from a single hinge. SWEET HOME was carved into it, and the remnants of some old bird-and-flower pattern. Sand was heaped up on the threshold. Deep footprints led inside.

We hesitated, a few yards away. The sun sank and the shadow fell across us.

"Mr. McNulty!" I softly called.

"We've brought some food, Mr. McNulty!" said Ailsa.

Nothing stirred down here. High above, a flight of

gannets headed north. A fox barked somewhere. The sea turned and groaned.

"We could just leave it in the doorway," I said.

"Yes," said Ailsa, and we moved forward again.

Then the curtain moved, his face appeared and we stood dead still. He stared. The lighthouse light swept past and lit the air above our heads.

"Come nearer, bonnies," said McNulty through the broken glass.

We didn't move.

"We brought you food and light," I said.

He stared. I wanted to drop our gifts, to grab Ailsa's hand, to run back home again. He raised his hand.

"This is the one I know," he said. He beckoned me. "Come closer, bonny lad." His face softened. "There was an angel at your side."

"Yes," I said. "I helped you. I held the casket, I collected money. It was in Newcastle, at the quay."

Ailsa held the package out.

"You must be so hungry," she said.

He closed his eyes.

"Yes," he said. "It is a time of great hunger, famine, waste and want." He tilted his head. "There it is. You hear it? You hear the wailing and weeping that's all around?"

"Yes," said Ailsa. "Mr. McNulty, will you eat the food we've brought?"

"Come inside, my bonnies. Come in through the door."

At first we didn't dare to move; then we caught each other's eye. We nodded. I lifted a stone as we crossed the threshold, waded through the deep soft sand there. There was a tiny dark hallway, then another door into the room where he waited for us. As we entered it I looked through the window and saw the final sliver of the sun go down.

Inside, everything was vague and lumpy: a mattress, a broken table, a ruined armchair. The floor was inches deep in sand. McNulty stood in the far corner.

"Be at home," he whispered. "McNulty will not scare you."

I lit the candles and stood them in the sand. Ailsa opened the package.

"They're jam tarts," she said. "And there's tea. Drink it while there's still some heat in it."

At first he wouldn't touch anything; then he crouched beside us and crammed the tarts into his mouth. He sighed at their sweetness. He gulped the tea. His face glowed in the candlelight.

"Such lovely bonny bairns," he said. He licked his lips. "I been eating seaweed. I been catching crabs and roasting them. I been glugging water from rain butts. But jam's the thing. Jam and tea."

I saw there was another window in the back wall of the room, but the dune had grown over it. Behind the glass were sand and soil and roots. There were seashells and stones and bones. He saw me looking.

"It's deep as the grave in here, bonny," he said. "We're down where the dead live. You want to see the needles and the skewer stuck in?"

He leapt for his casket, which lay in a corner on the sand.

"No," I said. "We need to go, Mr. McNulty."

I knew that people—Losh and Yak, my dad if he was able—would come searching for us now that McNulty lived beside us in the dunes.

He grabbed my wrist with bony fingers.

"You want to see the chains?"

I shook my head. I clenched my stone.

"Ailsa," I said.

He held me tighter.

"The world's afire!" he gasped.

We turned our faces to the shattered window. The sky above seemed filled with fire: great streaks of red and orange like flame and streaming lava.

"It's just the sunset," I said.

"Then what's all that weeping and that wailing, bonny?"

"It's just the sea, Mr. McNulty."

Ailsa touched him.

"Yes," she reassured him. "It's just the sea."

"We'll come back," I told him. "Take care. Be careful of who comes looking for you."

"Just the sea?" he said. He listened. "No, more than that." He held us for a moment. "Hurry home, children. Hurry to your beds and to your sleep. Oh, but then there's nightmares. What's to be done? Hurry home to your mummies and daddies and hold them close."

He let me go. We backed away. He came with us to the door. His face burned, a wild reflection of the sky. We hurried away into the deepening dusk.

"Get your shelters dug!" he yelled, as if to the whole world. "Dig down to where the dead live! Cover yourself with the earth. The world's afire! The sky's ablaze! There's no more night!"

We ran. His voice echoed after us. He howled like an animal in pain. We ran through the pines. We kept stumbling, and crashing into tree trunks. At last we reached the beach. We laughed together at the fear and excitement we felt. The lighthouse light swung beneath the fiery sky.

"Tomorrow," we whispered. "We'll take him more."

I rushed back to my homework.

Dad pressed his finger to his lips as I stumbled in.

"Hush, Bobby!" he hissed.

Neither he nor Mam took their eyes from the TV screen. There were pictures of nuclear missiles pointing at the sky. Then President Kennedy came on. He stared out at us. His gaze was calm.

"The world is on the abyss of destruction," he said.

His face disappeared. A nervous newscaster replaced him. He licked his lips. No one smiled.

"What's happening?" I said.

"Cuba," said Dad. He was racked with coughing. "Bloody Cuba."

✤ FORTY-ONE ✤

"This is Cuba," said Daniel. "This is the coast of America."

We were on the bus. He used his finger to draw in the condensation on the window. We perched on the seats around him: Diggy, Col, Ed and me. As he talked, others came closer: Doreen Armstrong and her friends, older kids.

"They're only ninety miles apart," said Daniel.

"Ninety miles!" said Col. "That's bloody miles, man. That's as far as . . ."

"Scotland!" said Diggy.

"Why, aye. Scotland," said Col.

Daniel just looked at them.

"Russia's put nuclear missiles into Cuba," he said. "They're pointing straight at the USA."

"USA?" said Col. "That's miles away and all."

"Far side of the world," said Diggy.

"And me dad says the USA's always too full of itself," said Ed.

"Why, aye," said Col.

Daniel shook his head. "What about the missiles in Russia pointing straight at us?"

Ed giggled.

"Mebbes they'll miss," he said. He arced his hand like a missile flying over us. "Splash! Straight into the Irish Sea."

"Aye," said Col. "Them Russians, man . . ."

Daniel shook his head again.

"Do you lot know nothing?" he said.

No one answered. We peered through Daniel's map into the sky.

"America's told Russia to get the missiles out of Cuba," said Daniel.

"And Russia's said hadaway and shite," said Diggy.

"And now," said Daniel, "there's Russian ships taking more missiles there, and America's told Russia to turn the ships back . . ."

"And Russia's said hadaway and shite," said Diggy.

"And now," said Daniel, "America's sent ships to stop the Russian ships and . . ."

Col stood up and made a pair of six-guns with his fingers, and drawled, "This ocean ain't big enough for the two of us."

Daniel looked at us all in amazement. "Do you lot not understand how dangerous it is?"

Diggy spat.

"Aye, Daniel, we do. So stop ganning on like that and stop goggling at us like that."

"Me dad was right," said Ed. "There's no point doing nowt."

"Once it starts...," said Col.

"Plenty missiles to destroy the whole world a dozen times over," said Diggy.

"All over the world they're getting ready," said Ed.

"Somebody'll press the button," said Col.

We looked into the sky.

Diggy spat again.

"Why the hell we going to school when this is going on?" he said.

Daniel wiped his map away. He pinned a CND badge on his lapel. The bus lurched toward the glass-and-redbrick building. We stared out at it.

"Bloody place," said Col.

FORTY-TWO

We knew they'd catch us in the end. We enticed them to us. We dropped photographs behind us as we walked through corridors. We left them in the corners of classrooms where we'd worked. We pinned them on notice boards and slotted them into the corners of picture frames and door frames. A couple of kids saw us, and the rumors smoldered through the school.

In the evening, the TV showed photographs of the weapons in Cuba, of the ships carrying more weapons, of American ships, of missiles and bombs and explosions. There were reports of riots. We saw CND protesters struggling with police in London, being arrested. Dad thumped the arm of his chair.

"Riot?" said Dad. "That's just people doing what they should do, making their voice heard, yelling out against what they know is wrong."

"Is it always right to protest," I said, "even if you think it's hopeless?"

"Aye," he said. "Especially then, when the odds seem stacked against you, when it seems you're yelling in the dark." We watched a young man thrown into the back of a Black Maria. "Even when it leads to trouble, like with that lad there. Leave that lad alone!"

The news ended. Dad turned to me.

"Everything that's been won for folks like us has been won by fighters, Bobby Burns. Fighters that wouldn't kowtow and cringe but looked the oppressors in the eye and said that things had to change."

He coughed. He sipped water. Did he seem frailer, smaller? Was the illness, whatever it was, taking him in its grip?

"Remember that," he said. "And remember there's times we need to keep on fighting still."

"I will," I said.

"Good lad."

We reached toward each other at the same time. Our hands met in the space between our chairs.

"Good lad," he said again.

"I love you, Dad," I said inside myself. "I love you. I love you."

Next day, I was all recklessness. My dad was ill. The world might be coming to an end. I wanted to stand up and fight before the darkness fell. All the way to school,

I felt the anger rising in me, I felt the strange joy of it all, the strange despair.

As we got off the bus, I took Daniel's arm.

"Mebbe this'll be our last day," I said.

"Maybe it will," he said.

We looked at each other.

"So what?" we said together.

"So let's do it properly," he said. "So let's do it boldly and bravely."

We gripped each other's hand, then we went into school and got on with it. Kids watched us, nudged each other, whispered about us. Bobby Burns, they said. Who'd believe it? Bobby Burns and Daniel Gower, that new kid from the South. It was me that brought it to an end. After lunch I put a photo onto Lubbock's desk. Everyone in the classroom saw me.

"It's true," said Dorothy Peacock. She stared. "It's really you."

I nodded.

"Aye. Me."

"And me," said Daniel.

Then Lubbock came in to register us. Deep silence. All the eyes of the others were upon us. Lubbock lifted the photograph between his finger and thumb as if it was a foul thing. He cast his eyes over us. He didn't need to say a word. I was trembling, my heart was thudding, my face was ablaze, but there was something inside me that was all delight. Daniel stood up. I stood up at his side.

"Me," said Daniel.

"Both of us," I said.

Lubbock sneered.

"So you're the scum," he said. He curled his finger. "Come with me."

❧ FORTY-THREE ❧

Grace's office. A crucifix and his doctorate from Leeds University hung side by side on the wall. There was a bunch of red flowers on a shelf. A statue of Our Lady stood in a little grotto carved into the wall. On his desk were a pile of Todd photographs, and his strap. His voice was quiet, almost tender.

"Robert Burns and Daniel Gower," he said. He smiled at Lubbock, who stood at our back. "An unlikely pairing, is it not, Mr. Lubbock?"

"Unlikely," he whispered. "But scum like these..."

"Yes," said Grace, "the lost and the fallen will find each other, no matter what their background."

I looked at Our Lady, at the snake that writhed in agony beneath her feet. I looked at Todd in his photograph, at the string of saliva caught between his bared teeth.

Grace flicked through a file.

"Your father," he said to me, "is in the yard."

"Yes," I said.

Lubbock jabbed me with his knuckle.

"Yes, sir," I said.

"And what will he make of all this?"

"I don't know, sir," I said.

"Don't know?"

"They don't care," said Lubbock. "That kind. The kind from Keely Bay..."

"The working classes," said Grace. "The lower orders. Perhaps it is a fantasy that they are ready for true education. What do you think, Burns?"

"Don't know, sir."

"Don't know? Then what would you say if your only outlook was to follow him into his yard?"

I looked down, then looked straight into his eye again.

"I wouldn't mind, sir," I said.

"Then perhaps it will be arranged. There are other places that will take you once we have finished with you here. Other places where the only outlook is the yard and places like the yard."

He flexed his strap between his hands.

"And you, Mr. Gower," he said, turning to Daniel. "I suspect that you are the true serpent in this garden. For you, of course, whatever happens, there is no prospect of the yard. There are places that will fall over themselves to take you. Your father—"

"He helped me," said Daniel suddenly. "He printed the photographs."

"Yes, of course he did." Grace spread his hands and smiled at me. "There is a nest of vipers living by you on your beach, Robert Burns. They have poisoned you with their venom. They have led you astray."

"Led you into sin," whispered Lubbock. "Led you right up to the devil's door."

"Did you imagine that this boy could be your friend?" said Grace. "Did you imagine that once you were caught, and once you were dealt with, that this boy would be true to you? No, Robert Burns. This boy's affections and his loyalties will blow with the wind. You are his plaything. You will be in your yard, in your overalls, staring out through its iron gates, and your friend here, Mr. Gower, will be outside with his camera. He will make such a pretty picture of you behind your bars. He will show such disappointment in your eyes. He will suggest such a yearning in your heart. He will catch such pain in your expression, and in your posture. Yours will make such an appealing picture for the higher orders, Robert Burns."

Daniel clicked his tongue.

"He's talking rubbish. Don't let him scare you, Bobby."

Lubbock jabbed him in the ribs. Grace suddenly

reached across the desk and ripped the CND badge from Daniel's lapel.

"You can't do that," said Daniel. He pointed at the photographs. "And you can't do that. It's wrong to hit children."

Grace flushed.

"Is this what your father says?"

"It's what my father knows."

"Fortunately, in this place, we hold to other beliefs."

Grace lifted the strap and stood up and came round the desk toward us.

"Don't touch me," said Daniel.

Grace reached out to him.

"You dare to command me? Stand still, boy!" he hissed.

Daniel turned away to leave but Lubbock held him.

"This is a cowardly worm!" said Lubbock. "Tough enough to do the dirty secret deeds but too scared to take any punishments."

Daniel twisted free. He spat on the floor.

"And you are fascist pigs. Come on," he said. "Just leave, Bobby."

"Stand still!" said Grace.

I couldn't move. I knew that I should just run with Daniel, but I couldn't move. Lubbock tried to restrain Daniel again, but Grace shook his head.

"Let him go, Mr. Lubbock. It is the last time he will be seen in this place."

Daniel hesitated in the doorway. He looked me in the eye.

"I'll see you on the beach tonight, Bobby," he said. He clenched his fists. "What we did was right. You know that. Remember that."

Then he was gone.

Grace smiled.

"As I said. So the serpent slithers off. Now, then, Robert Burns."

I held out my hand; then there was a soft knocking at the door. Lubbock opened it. Todd stepped inside.

"Here is your tormentor," said Grace. He held out the strap to Todd. "Would you care to . . . ?"

But Todd shook his head.

"No, thank you, sir," he murmured. "This is your domain."

He looked at me, this little cruel stupid man. I don't think he even recognized me. He quickly looked away.

"You must apologize," said Grace.

I said nothing.

"You must say sorry to Mr. Todd, and you must mean it," said Grace.

I held out my hand. I said nothing. I thought of Dad. Make him better, I whispered to myself. Take all the pain away from him.

"Apologize."

My lips stayed shut.

The strap whipped down. I gasped with pain. Tears

filled my eyes. I looked directly back at Grace as the strap whipped down again. I was a fighter. I could take any pain he gave me. His punishment would only make me stronger. He told me again to apologize. My lips stayed shut.

✖ FORTY-FOUR ✖

I was told that the bishop would be informed about these incidents. He would help decide my future. The staff of the school would meet to discuss my case. I should stay at home until I was sent for. I should make a confession to my local priest. I should describe my wrongdoing to my parents. I should contemplate the harm I had caused to Mr. Todd, to the community of the school, to my own prospects, and to my soul. I was given a letter to take home. As he wrote it, in his brisk black script, Grace paused and looked up at me.

"Do your parents read well enough?" he asked.

I wanted to grab his strap and attack him in reply. I trembled with frustration and pain. Through the window, I saw Miss Bute watching from beyond the car park, her head tilted to one side, her chin in her hand. Grace pressed the letter onto blotting paper and folded it into an envelope. "You have a final opportunity to apologize," he said. My lips stayed shut. I took the letter and backed away, out of the office, into the corridor. I hurried through the school. Kids goggled from their classrooms. I saw teachers trying to compose them for their work. I heard their yells. I imagined their words: Don't look. That boy is no example for you. See what happens to those who wander into sin. I ran from the front door and felt such freedom, such triumph. I rubbed my hands and the pain was soon gone. My mind was all astorm. I did some kind of crazy dance in the yard before I ran from the school grounds into the cold October afternoon. I ran homeward, taking the bus route, running on pavements, then on a roadside verge, then through the birch and pine and hawthorn woods that lined the road. The sky was filled with larks and gulls. I sang myself, like some weird bird, whistling and yowling and waving my arms. I smelt the sea and heard the sea and saw the summit of the distant lighthouse. The land glowed beneath the low sun: corn stubble and brown earth and fiery leaves and the sky was icy blue. I ran through dark shadows and into dazzling beams of light. I yelled my delight:

"Freedom! Freedom! Destroy the missiles! Save the world! Save my dad!"

I felt that I could run all day, that I could run for my whole life. I ran past the Rat and the post office and the scattered houses and down the lane to the beach and toward the sea and I slowed as I approached the house. I waded through the sand. I unlatched the gate. I took deep breaths. I trembled. What would they say, when so many of their hopes and dreams were lodged in me? I went inside. No one there. Just emptiness. A fire shrinking in the grate. A cold pot of tea. Then I found the scribbled note.

We're at the hospital. Back soon. Mam. x.

I ripped off my uniform. I pulled on old clothes. I gabbled something at Mary and Bernadette. I stabbed a needle into the flesh between my finger and thumb.

"Please," I whispered. "No! Bloody no!"

Then I calmed myself. I stared out from my window. Down on the shoreline, Joseph was building a bonfire. He was bare-chested. Further south, half a mile away along the beach, the Spinks were in the water getting coal. I saw Ailsa's silhouette dancing on the cart, Losh and Yak and Mr. Spink wielding their massive shovels. The late sunlight glinted off them, the silvery sea gleamed all around them. To the north, from among the dunes, the smoke of McNulty's little fire snaked into the late-afternoon air. The sky above us all was empty but for birds and clouds.

I went downstairs. I added my own note to theirs.

I'm on the beach. B. x.

❧ FORTY-FIVE ❧

"Joseph," I called, but he didn't hear.

He was bowed forward; he carried great timbers across his bare shoulders. He dragged them away from me, toward the huge pile down by the shoreline.

"Joseph!" I yelled, and he turned at last.

He dropped the timbers and laughed and came to me.

"Bobby Burns! What you doing out this time of day?"

My feet shifted on the sand at the excitement of saying it:

"They hoyed me out, Joseph."

"You? Bobby Burns?"

"Me, Joseph, and they might not let me back!"

His eyes widened at the amazement of it.

"But what you done, Bobby?"

"Oh...everything!"

He came and held my face in his hands.

"But what about university and all that stuff?" he said. "What about the future?"

"What future, Joseph?"

Then he whispered, "Look!" and he turned around, and I saw that the whole of his dragon had been filled in. Blood still marked the needle points. There was bruising under the garish greens and golds and reds of the beast's body. There were horns and warts. The claws gripped Joseph's sides, the tail whipped down beneath his ice-blue jeans. Flames belched from the open jaws, they flared across the back of his neck, licked toward his throat and beneath his hairline. The dragon seemed like part of him, something growing out from him.

"Isn't it bloody wonderful?" he said.

I reached out and touched it gently and felt how soft his skin was and how tender it was.

"Was agony!" he said.

A tiny scab broke off beneath my touch.

"Should still have it covered up," he said. "Got to keep it clean. But what the hell?"

He turned to me again.

"It's beautiful," I said.

"Dad stuffed a wad of notes into me hand yesterday. Gan on, he says. Get the whole lot done at once. No point waiting for nothing now. It took hours! Now I'm getting the bonfire ready. Been doing it all day. It'll be the biggest ever." He spread his arms against the sky to show how massive it would be. "We'll not wait for Guy Fawkes Night this year. Set it off early, eh?"

"Aye!"

He laughed loudly.

"They're gonna blast us all to smithereens so there'll be no Guy Fawkes Night anyway! Help us, Bobby?"

"Aye," I said.

We searched the beach and its hinterland for timber. We dragged logs and dried-out seaweed and fish boxes and tires from the jetsam. There were fence posts and gates in the sand, remnants of disappeared gardens. We dragged fallen branches from among the pines. We went to where the shacks were. We found fallen roof timbers, ruined armchairs, floorboards and doors: anything that was old, anything that was dilapidated. Over the hill of sand, McNulty's smoke continued to rise. We stood for a moment and watched but we didn't go to him.

"Been dreaming about him," said Joseph. "Been dreaming that I touch the fire, that I feel nothing, that I'm him."

He tilted his head and breathed powerfully out, as if there was a fire roaring from his throat.

"I want to learn it from him," he said. "To hell with being a builder!" He laughed. "I want to be a fire-eater!"

We hauled our discoveries back to the shoreline and heaped them up and flung them high. We worked and

sweated and cursed and laughed and I tried to think of
nothing but being with Joseph Connor as I'd been with
him so many times since I'd been born. Then we rested.
Joseph lit a cigarette and grimaced and grinned at the
pains in his back. I looked back toward home and saw
no movement there. I trembled and my fears for Dad
and my memories of the awful time in Grace's office
came streaming back. I couldn't control myself and I
cried and Joseph put an arm around me and I told him
about Todd and Daniel and the school and my dad and
I leaned on him, Joseph Connor, the boy I'd known
since I was born, the greatest friend I'd had, who'd always been something like a brother. He told me I'd
done right and my dad would be fine but I couldn't stop
the tears running from my eyes, I couldn't stop the feel-
ing of helplessness and uselessness.

"I feel that little," I said. "And everything's that big
and there's nothing I can do and—"

"What way's that to talk?" he said. "That's not what
we expect from the lad that took on the devil of Sacred
Heart."

He pulled me to my feet.

"Howay, Bobby, man!" he said. "At least you can yell
and scream and stamp your feet and build a fire high as
bloody heaven and you can yell out, No, bloody no, I
won't put up with it!"

He glared into my eyes, and his face shone red beneath the reddening sky.

"No!" he yelled, and I clenched my fists and joined in with him.

"No! No! Bloody no!"

"Aye!" he said. "At least make a noise. At least say, I'm me! I'm Bobby Burns! At least if the worst comes to the worst you can say I been here, I existed!"

The Spinks had finished their coal gathering and they headed toward us as we stamped and yelled. The dark and beautiful knotted shape of the family waded the edge of the turning surf.

"Aye, aye!" shouted Yak as they came closer. "It's yelling Brains and Dragonback and a bloody great big fire! Here, have this!" he shouted as they came close by, and he flung a bucketful of soaking sea coal onto our heap. "This'll make the heart as hot as hell."

"Hope you're not waiting for Guy Fawkes Night," said Losh, " 'cos there'll be no bloody Guy Fawkes Night."

Joseph laughed at him.

"Heard the news?" he said.

"Aye," said Losh. "And it's nowt but bad."

"No, the real news. Our Bobby's been chucked out of school!"

"No!" said Yak.

"Diven't believe it!" said Losh.

"Tell them, Bobby," said Joseph.

All their eyes were on me. The words stuck in my throat. Ailsa sat on her perch on top of the coal and looked me in the eye and knew that it was true. I nodded at her: Aye.

Losh thumped his shovel on the wheel of the cart.

"Howay," he said. "Get up on this cart and we'll ride down to that school and sort the toerags out reet now. Who we gunning for? Who we going to hoy on top of the fire?"

"It's the new kid," said Joseph. "It's his doing."

"Might've known," said Losh. He picked up his shovel. "Ponces from the South. Howay, let's gan and get him."

"Now, then, lads," said Mr. Spink. He stood with his arm around Wilberforce. "Do your mam and dad know, Bobby?"

I shook my head.

"They're at the hospital," I muttered, and Ailsa jumped down and came to my side and hugged me and something roared far far away and we all stood dead still and didn't dare to breathe till the noise was gone.

"They're home, Bobby," said Joseph.

And I turned and saw the lights on, and a dark figure moving about inside.

✖ FORTY-SIX ✖

I shuffled slowly, silently through the sand. Hardly made a sound as I opened the front door. Hardly breathed. Not a soul in the living room. The fire'd been heaped up. I heard them moving in the kitchen. The smell of bacon frying, the sound of the kettle boiling. Mam started singing.

"Oh, weel may the keel row,
The keel row, the kee-el row.
Oh, weel may the keel row,
That my true laddie's in..."

Then hummed the same tune again, higher and sweeter. She laughed.
"Can you not wait till it's on your plate?"
Dad smacked his lips.
"Delicious!" he said.

Then silence from them, then softer voices.

"You big daft man," she said. She giggled. "Go and see if you can find our Bobby. Tell him it's on the table now."

He came out of the kitchen, stood in the doorway.

"Talk of the devil," he said. "And he's black as the roads. What you been doing out there, lad?"

I blinked. Couldn't speak. He grinned.

"He's lost his tongue and all!"

"Dad," I said.

"That's me."

"Are you OK?" I said.

"Never better."

She came to his back. She drew her hair from her face and smiled at me.

"But...," I said.

"But what?" he said.

"But your coughing, and all the tests, and..."

"They found nowt."

"Nowt?"

"Just like I knew they would. Nowt. Just like I knew all along."

"But... But..."

Mam nodded.

"It's true," she said. "Nothing at all."

"Mebbes a bug or something, eh?" he said. "Mebbes a little passing germ that's flown away and's looking for another body to land in for a while." She put her arms around him. "Now, then," he said. "Go and wash that muck off, else I'll be eating yours and all."

I went to the bathroom. I tugged out splinters from my hands and arms. They left little bulbs of blood on my skin. I washed with creamy white soap and scrubbed all the dirt away. The lighthouse light passed across the window, once, twice, three times. I looked into my empty pupils, black as night. I tried to think but had no thoughts to think.

"Thank you," I whispered. There was no answer. Maybe there was no one to answer. Maybe there was just nothing, going on forever and forever. Out there on the beach, someone laughed, maybe Losh, maybe Yak. Then Ailsa's ringing voice. "Thank you," I said again.

"Bobby!" Dad called. "I'm starting in on yours!"

We sat around the table, eating our bacon and eggs and tomatoes and swigging mugs of tea. Mam hummed "The Keel Row." Dad wrapped a slice of bacon in a slice of bread and chewed it and licked the fat that ran down to his chin. Sometimes we laughed gently. Mam said they'd had to wait an age to get a bus out of town, then there wasn't a seat to be found. She was going to complain and get that service sorted out. "It's getting beyond a joke," she said. She kept topping the mugs up with tea. Dad grinned and grinned at the pleasures of his food, at the pleasures of being with his family. The rattle of the cart and the shadow of the Spinks moved past. I saw Ailsa's glinting eyes look quickly in at us.

When they'd gone, Joseph's bonfire stood like a mountain before the sea.

Mam leaned over and kissed me.

"So, bonny lad," she said at last. "How was school today?"

And I searched for a lie to tell but could find none.

❦ FORTY-SEVEN ❦

I bowed my head as I told the tale. I looked up when it was over.

"So it was all that Daniel's idea?" said Mam.

"It was my own idea to join him."

"And this Mr. Todd. Surely he can't be—"

"Yes, he can," said Dad. "I've known plenty fellers like your Mr. Todd."

Mam stroked my head.

"You," she said. "Why d'you make everything so hard for yourself?"

Dad tapped my skull.

"Too much going on in there, that's why."

"And why didn't you come and tell us?"

"I'm sorry," I said.

"For what you did?" he said.

I sighed.

"No," I told him.

"Good lad. We didn't fight a war so that berks like your Mr. Todd could hold sway."

They looked at each other.

"There's more to education than reading books and scribbling in books," said Dad. "There's ancient battles to be fought."

She clicked her tongue.

"Battles!" she murmured.

"Aye," he said. "You know it as well as I do, and you know this lad's got right on his side."

We put the TV on for the news. When it came we trembled. The Russian ships had not turned back. America was ready to sink them. All U.S. nuclear forces were on alert. It was assumed that the Russians were ready too.

Dean Rusk, the American secretary of state, was interviewed.

"We're in as grave a crisis as mankind has ever been in," he said.

"We must try to stay calm," he said.

He chewed his lips.

"We're standing at the gates of hell," he said.

Mam held me tight.

"You wouldn't be going to school anyway," she said. "Not in these dark days."

Afterward, we just sat close together, leaned slightly against each other. The sea boomed. The fire hissed in the grate. Daylight faded.

"How much warning will there be?" said Mam.

"A few minutes," I said. "A few seconds."

"None," said Dad.

I saw Joseph's silhouette struggling toward the bonfire across the beach. The lighthouse light moved across him.

Mam held me tighter.

"Stay inside," she whispered.

✵ FORTY-EIGHT ✵

Couldn't sleep that night. As if the whole world couldn't sleep. I sat beside the Lourdes light. My own reflection gazed fearfully back at me. I made a funnel of my hands, and peered through myself. I watched the turning light, and as I watched, the light began to slow. It inched across the sea toward the land. Then stopped, dead still. And then went out. And for the first time ever, our lighthouse light was dark and still. Breath was shallow, heart was slow and light. From the room next door, not a sound. I imagined them lying there together, hands linked, eyes half open, listening, waiting.

I ripped some pages from my notebook and I wrote.

Keely Bay. It's a tiny corner of the world. It's nothing to the universe. A tatty place, a coaly beach by a coaly sea. I know that we don't matter. Maybe nothing matters. Whatever happens the stars will go on shining and the sun will go on shining and the world will go on spinning through the blackness and the emptiness. But it's where I live and where the people I love live and where the things I love live. My mam and dad. Ailsa Spink and Mr. Spink and Losh and Yak. Wilberforce the pony. The miraculous fawn. Joseph Connor and his mam and dad. Daniel Gower and his mam and dad, McNulty in the dunes. The crabs and limpets and snails that live in the rock pools, the anemones and starfish and seaweed, the rocks, the water, the shoals of fish that live in the sea, the seals, the dolphins we see sometimes, the jelly-fish, every single grain of sand, every single grain of coal. The rickety beach café, the Rat, the post office, the pines, the lighthouse, the swinging lighthouse light, the dunes, the shacks. Foxes and badgers and deer and rats and voles and moles and worms and centipedes and the adders that we see on the paths in summer, and the bees and wasps and butter-flies and midges. Crows and linnets and skylarks and gulls. Chickens and eggs and peas and tomatoes and raspberries. Chrysanthemums, hawthorn, holly, birch. I can't name everything, but save them. If these things can be saved, then maybe everything can be saved. Save Diggy, Col and Ed and Doreen. Save Lubbock, Todd and Grace. Save good Miss Bute. Take me. If somebody has to be taken, take me. I live in Keely Bay beside the lighthouse, near to everything I love. I'm in the window with the Lourdes light. My name is Bobby Burns. Take me.

❧ FORTY-NINE ❧

The sun woke me. It was sludgy yellow, slithering over the edge of the sea. My head was on my arm. My body ached. I scanned the world for fire, for cascading dust, but there was nothing. I folded my notebook pages, shoved them in my pocket and went downstairs. I put the kettle on. Mam came soundlessly behind me in bare feet and put her arms around me.

"Good morning, Rebel Heart," she said.

Then Dad. He hugged us. He switched the radio on and it told us an American plane had been shot down over Cuba and...He simply switched it off again. He breathed deeply and tapped his chest. Chucking the tabs would save him a fortune, he said. He'd start saving for holidays now. She laughed and said, So we're heading for Australia! Mebbes Scarborough, he said. We had breakfast. He crunched his toast and said he was looking forward to work again. He winked. And getting this lad back to school again. And getting the roof fixed, said Mam, and getting a lick of paint on the doors before winter, and getting the draft-proofing done again, and...She told me to eat but I couldn't eat. I licked some honey from a spoon she held out to me. I sipped some tea from a cup she held up to me. She called me lovely boy. She called Dad lovely man. She started to sing "The Keel Row," but she stopped halfway through and we all listened to the world but there was nothing.

"We'll go out," she said, so we all put boots and coats on and we went out onto the beach. We walked through the soft coaly sand and the line of rubbish and jetsam and the firm wet sand beyond. We laughed at the size of Joseph's bonfire, and we saw other distant bonfires, heaped on the beaches before the little villages and settlements to the south.

Soon Joseph came to us, carrying yet more timbers. He yelled out a good morning.

"Old floorboards," he told us. "Me dad was going to use them again but what the hell?"

He couldn't resist lifting his shirt, showing his dragon.

"But did it not hurt, son?" said Mam.

"It bloody knacked, Mrs. Burns. But look, man. Wasn't it worth it?"

He lowered his shirt again, and tipped his head toward me.

"Things is OK?" he said.

"Aye, things is OK," said Dad.

Joseph laughed. He rolled his eyes.

"What a kid! Fancy getting chucked out in his first term. I doubt even Losh Spink managed that." He started to move away, then half turned. "You'll be around all day?" he said.

"Aye," we said.

"Aye. That's good, eh?" he said, and he walked on to his fire.

We went nowhere very far: as far as the pines and back again, as far as the beach café, as far as the hawthorn lanes. We walked around the lighthouse and we stepped across the rock pools. We walked circles and spirals and figures of eight. The world stayed still. No wind. The tide moved in but the waves were tiny things that splashed almost silent on the shore. Gulls called and birds sang but their voices were frail like something from a dream. Joseph went on working, building his fire toward heaven. We couldn't stop ourselves from pausing, listening. We couldn't stop expecting hell.

We all just laughed when we saw Wilberforce. Here he came, unfettered, uncarted, trotting awkwardly down onto the beach. He snorted and kicked the sand. He stepped into the fringe of the sea and splashed. The Spinks came after him. They wore clean clothes and their faces were shining. They strolled like holiday-makers and waved when they saw us, and our two families moved toward each other.

"You're OK, then?" said Mr. Spink.

"Never better," answered Dad.

Mr. Spink eyed him, checking the truth of what he'd said.

"That's good. But all the rest's a bad do, eh?"

"It is," said Dad.

"And we thought the last one was the last one, eh?"

The two men approached each other. They shook hands and quickly held each other's shoulders.

"We've been all right," said Dad softly.

"We have," said Mr. Spink. He scanned the sea and sky. "Ha! Will you look at that daft pony!"

Ailsa came to my side and guided me away from the others. She was carrying her fawn in a cardboard box. It lay there contentedly on a bed of straw and looked up at us, so trusting.

"So it was nowt, then?" said Ailsa. "With your dad."

"Aye, it was nowt." I looked sideways into her eyes. "Or it was you."

"Or you, Bobby, and the things we said."

I reached down and stroked the fawn.

"Aye," I said. "And all the things that we don't understand."

She put the box down on the beach. She held my hand.

"Want to be with you all day long," she said. "I don't want to go out of your sight."

We walked.

"Don't worry, little fawn," she said. "We'll not be far away."

We wandered. We watched Joseph. Dad and Mam and Mr. Spink talked about the old days. Losh and Yak rode poor Wilberforce through the water, clinging to his mane as if he was a wild stallion; then they let him lie in the soft sand and they stroked him and whispered to him. All of us kept turning to each other, as if checking that each of us was there. My mind kept slipping, drifting. I saw myself as a little boy again, running to the water with my bucket and spade. I saw myself tumbling and squealing and being bowled over by the waves. I saw Mam picking me up and comforting me and putting me in the water again. I saw the three of us down there, Mam and Dad in stripy deck chairs, me building sand castles. I saw Ailsa toddling toward us hand in hand with her mam, and I saw again how lovely Mrs. Spink had been. I saw Joseph wrestling with me, grunting and growling and telling me how hard he'd make me. I saw Keely Bay as it had been all through my childhood, hardly changing apart from getting more tattered and worn. I know that Ailsa saw such things as well. Maybe all of us saw such things, for all of us kept entering such deep silences. We were surrounded by the ghosts of who we'd been before and who we'd known before. Outside us in the world, nothing happened, nothing happened. I went further back. I saw Dad as he had been in his boyhood photographs. I saw him on the beach. I saw him truly, for he stood at the water's edge as real and solid as me, and I know I could almost have touched him; then he turned around and looked me in the eye. He smiled, he waved, I blinked, and he was gone.

As we walked, sometimes Ailsa and I murmured our prayers together. We wished and wished: *Don't let it happen. Keep us safe.* Sometimes when I reeled and slipped, and lost connection with the world around, I thought it must be the beginning of my death. I thought that this might be how it felt when my own prayers began to work, when I was taken as a sacrifice. I walked out with Ailsa to the rocks below the lighthouse and looked down into the deep dark sea. I stared along the beach to Joseph's waiting bonfire. I caught my breath and trembled. Maybe I wouldn't be taken. Maybe I had to give myself, to throw myself into water or fire, to lose myself in scorching heat or icy cold. "Not too close, Bobby," said Ailsa, drawing me back from the brink. "Are you all right?" she said. "No," I answered. "Are you?" She shook her head. We smiled at each other. How could we be all right?

Mam laid blankets on the sand. She brought food out for us all. Scones and bread and butter and cheese and golden syrup. Losh dashed home and brought a crate of beer. We spread ourselves out on the sand and ate and drank. Joseph came and ate hungrily. He reached out and took a bottle of beer and swigged from it and wiped his lips with his fist like a man. Ailsa let the fawn lick butter from her fingers. Wilberforce nibbled the grass nearby. As we sat there, Daniel and his parents came out of their house. They paused and watched us for a while, then came shyly on. They carried some bottles of wine. Losh and Yak and Joseph watched them coldly.

"What they wanting with us?" muttered Losh.

But Mam stood up and greeted them and drew them in. Dad shook hands with Mr. Gower.

"There's a bit of sorting out to do, I hear," he said.

Mr. Gower shrugged.

"Yes," he said.

"Seems we got a pair of fighters on our hands," said Dad.

Mr. Gower looked at us.

"Maybe because they were brought up in similar ways," he said.

He pulled the cork from a bottle of wine, handed it to Dad, and Dad smiled and swigged.

Mam beckoned Mrs. Gower.

"Come and sit," said Mam. "Make yourself at home."

Daniel came to my side.

"Did they strap you?" he said.

I nodded and showed him the marks.

"And we're both kicked out?"

I nodded again.

"One day," he said, "there'll be a law against the things they do."

"Oh, aye?" I said.

"Oh, aye." He laughed at himself using the strange word. "Aye. Oh, aye." Then he asked, "Are you keeping up with things?"

He started to draw a map in the sand: Cuba, the USA, where the ships were now. Did we know a plane had been shot down? Had we heard—

"Stop it," I said.

I swept his map away. I knelt there and hung my head and expected to be struck down at any moment.

"Just stop it!"

❧ FIFTY ❧

It was Mam who said we should bring McNulty.

"That poor soul," she said. "Who'd be alone on a day like this?"

"It'll need to be Bobby that goes," said Ailsa. "I'll go with him."

We saw the fear in Mam's eyes, in everyone's eyes.

"We'll be fast," I said. "Five minutes, no more."

We stood up in the silence. We scanned the sky. And then we ran. Dad came with us as far as the pines. He stood at the edge of the dunes, below the hill of sand, and watched us climb. We lay side by side at the top and looked down on McNulty's shack. His fire was out. Sand was heaped on it. No movement, no signs of life. I waved to Dad and we crawled over and slithered down.

"Mr. McNulty!" I called.

Nothing stirred. We went to the window but couldn't see through the tattered curtain. We called his name from the door. We went inside, over the heaped-up sand at the threshold. We pushed open the door to the inner room. He was there, below the window filled with sand and roots and skeletons. He whimpered in fright.

"It's me," I said. "It's Bobby. I helped you, Mr. McNulty. Remember?"

"Get back to your shelters!" he hissed. "Stay still. Stay quiet. Get down where the dead are!"

"We've come to help you," Ailsa said. "We've got food and drink waiting."

"There's people there," I said. "They want you to be with them."

"People!" His eyes were shining. "People! Get them underground, bonny. Cover them up."

I crouched beside him.

"There's no point to it," I said. "There's nowhere safe, nowhere to hide." I put my hand on his skinny elbow. "Please come with us."

"Please," echoed Ailsa.

I held him.

"These people will care for you," I whispered.

"Care?" he said.

"Will love you," I said.

I smiled.

"And you could perform for them," I said. "You could do your act for them, Mr. McNulty."

He whimpered again. He closed his eyes.

"Oh, bonny," he whispered. He gripped my hand. "Oh, what are you saying, my bonny boy?"

❄ FIFTY-ONE ❄

McNulty hung his chains around his shoulders. I carried his box of instruments, his torches, his bottle of kerosene, his sack on a stick. Ailsa held his elbow and guided him. We climbed away from the shack. We encouraged him, we told him who was waiting, we told him that everything would turn out fine. He didn't make a sound. The sun was already descending toward the moors in the west.

Dad clenched his fists with relief when he saw us.

"McNulty!" he said as we approached. He took McNulty by the shoulders and looked into his eyes. "It's grand to see you again, McNulty."

"It's my dad," I murmured. "Do you remember?"

But we saw that he remembered nothing.

We walked through the shadows of the pines, past the lighthouse, past the bonfire, toward the group of neighbors. We saw that Joseph's parents had come to join us as well now.

"This is where we live," I said. "Keely Bay. That's our house there. These are the people who live here. This is my mam." She stood up and came toward us. "She was with me when I saw you first. Do you remember her, Mr. McNulty?" He hesitated on the sand, narrowed his eyes, and I saw that yes, maybe he did remember. "She was the angel at my side," I said. He sighed and closed his eyes as she came close to him. She took his arm. "Come and be with us, Mr. McNulty," she said, and he let her lead him further.

He knelt in the sand beside her and took bread and cheese from her. He drank beer. He kept his eyes turned downward. The others watched him, uncertain. It was as if all their dread had been disturbed by the presence of this stranger in our midst.

"This is Mr. McNulty," I said. "He's an escapologist and a fire-eater."

"The greatest of the fire-eaters," said Ailsa.

McNulty sighed.

"In the greatest of the fire-eaters," he said, "you cannot see where the . . ."

He ran out of words, stumbled into a silence in which we remembered our dread again and we stared into the sky and we listened.

"What's next?" whispered McNulty. "The fire or the chains or . . ." He got up awkwardly, he stood there, he caught my eye, he groaned. "Help me, bonny?"

I stood beside him.

"Fasten my chains."

I started to unwind the chains from around his shoulders, to wrap them around his body.

"Tighter!" he whispered. "Tighter, bonny!"

I wrapped them tighter. I wrapped them around his arms, his legs. I intertwined and knotted them. There were little padlocks that I snapped shut. All the time he told me, "Tighter! Tighter!"

I wrapped the last section of chain around his throat.

"Pay!" he said. He glared out at his audience. He glared at me. "The sack, bonny. Tell them to put their coins in it. Tell them they'll not see nowt till they pay."

I lifted the sack on the stick and I held it out. The others fiddled in their pockets for coins.

"Pay!" he said. "D'you think a man like me can live on empty air?"

Soon a few coins were in the sack.

"Enough! To hell with them," he said.

He dropped to the earth. He squirmed and jerked and gasped and started to slither free of the chains. We chewed our lips at the horror of this happening on our beach today. We laughed at the stupidity of it, the madness of it. We shed tears at the sadness of it. Then he was free, and kneeling on the sand with his head hanging low.

"See?" he said. "See what a man can do?"

We stared into the sky. It was reddening, darkening. McNulty gasped as if in agony.

"What's the wailing?" he said.

"The sea," I told him. "Nothing but the sea."

He put his hands across his ears.

"Stop the wailing!" he said. "Stop that screaming! Oh, what's to be done about the doom that's everywhere?"

He reached out, grabbed me.

"The box!" he said. "Get the box, bonny. Get the thing that'll make the most pain."

I opened the box and took out the silver skewer with the fierce pointed tip, the handle a Saracen's head. "Who would dare?" he asked. No one answered. He told nobody to pay. He pushed it through his cheeks and we gathered in front of him to see the metal stretched between his teeth, across his throat, to see it gleaming there in the last fiery rays of the setting sun.

❧ FIFTY-TWO ❧

Mam sang when the sun had gone.

"Oh, weel may the keel row,
The keel row, the kee-el row,
Oh, weel may the keel row,
That my true laddie's in."

Mr. Gower poured her a glass of wine.

"Thank you," she said. "You didn't bring your camera today, Paul?"

He shook his head.

"Not today."

"So you have all you need for your book?"

"There'll be more, Mrs. Burns, once this is over."

"Once this is over," growled Joseph softly, imitating Mr. Gower's southern vowels.

"Do you really like it here, Paul?" said Mam. She looked into his eyes. "Or are you just using us?"

"It is very beautiful, Mrs. Burns. We're very pleased that we came."

"Oh, weel may the keel row,
The keel row, the kee-el row..."

McNulty lay silent in the sand, curled up, apart from us. It grew dark. The moon didn't rise. The lighthouse light didn't turn. Nothing but stars, the impossible number of them looking down, and the endless reflections of them on the sea. Then Ailsa saw the single light among them, moving slowly from the east. "Look," she whispered, and she pointed, and we traced it with our eyes in silence.

"It'll be Sputnik," said Daniel.

It passed over us. We breathed.

"What did the satellite say to the moon?" said Yak.

"Dunno," someone answered.

"Can't stop," said Yak. "I'm Russian."

"Fire time," said Joseph. "Let's not wait for Guy Fawkes Night."

"Guy Fawkes Night!" said Losh, and he jumped up and he and Joseph and Yak ran full speed to the fire and we saw the matches sparking there and the first flames burning.

McNulty didn't come with us. Mam laid a blanket over him.

"God bless," she whispered.

I crouched beside him for a moment.

"You OK?" I said.

He caught my hand. His eyes softened.

"Aye," he said, and for a moment all the madness seemed gone from him. He looked at me tenderly. "Don't be troubled," he said. "I love you, bonny." Then he closed his eyes and I followed the others to the shoreline. The great fire quickly began to roar. The fires to the south began to burn as well, making a row of fires at the edge of the land and sea. We had to back away from the heat. Joseph put his arm around me.

"Watch it burn as high as heaven, Bobby," he said.

He kissed me suddenly, secretly.

Mam asked us to pray.

"Even if you don't believe," she said. "Even if you think there's nothing but nothing."

So we knelt there, all of us, beside the fire and the water and we sent our voices upward with the flames.

"Don't let it happen," I said with Ailsa. "Please. Please."

I took my prayer from my pocket and threw it into the fire and it leapt upward as it blazed.

Then we sat in pairs and little groups and hardly spoke and the grown-ups drank beer and wine and I lay sleeping for a while and when I woke I found Daniel and Ailsa sitting together close by. They were talking about Kent and Keely Bay and schools and mothers and fawns and how they loved freedom and how they hated being told what to do and I lay listening to their voices, that were both so quiet and strong and yet so different from each other, and I knew that if we could just get through these days and nights of dread a time of great excitement might be waiting for us all. And as I lay there I half opened my eyes to look at my friends and I saw the fire-eater far beyond them in the darkness, all alone, breathing his flag of flame into the air. No one else had seen. The grown-ups faced the fire and the sea. I crawled to Daniel and Ailsa.

"Look," I whispered.

And they turned, and we shuffled silently away from the fire and into the deeper dark and we sat together there and we saw how marvelous McNulty was and how his face blazed like his fire and how when he ate his fire we couldn't tell where the fire ended and the man began. And perhaps he saw us, too, and recognized the children who had discovered him and drawn him here and who had tried to care for him and love him, for he spread his torches wide as if in greeting; then he breathed his fire again, breathed it out, then breathed it in.

✾ FIFTY-THREE ✾

If. If Kennedy or Khrushchev had given the order to launch the missiles that night... If some general in some bunker under the earth, or some commander of a submarine deep down in the sea, or some pilot of some plane, had gone mad with the pressure of it all and stabbed the launch button all alone... If some primitive computer had simply gone wrong... If the ships heading for Cuba had continued heading for Cuba. If... If... I'd not be sitting here beside the old Lourdes light writing the story. There'd be no record of what happened in Keely Bay during that autumn of 1962. Maybe there'd be no record of what happened anywhere in autumn 1962. Maybe there'd be nothing, no world at all, just a charred and blasted ball of poisoned earth and poisoned air and poisoned seas, spinning through the darkness and the emptiness of space. All of history gone. All the stories gone. No me, no you, no anyone. But no one pressed the launch button. The ships turned back. We stepped back from the gates of hell.

All over the world, people behaved the way we did in little tattered Keely Bay. We trembled and quaked and were filled with dread. We shouted, No! Of course, there were riots and looting in some places. Even close to home in Newcastle there was fighting in the streets. A bunch of kids set fire to a newsagent's in Blyth. But most of us, as in Keely Bay, stayed together and fed each other and tried to love each other. Even those of us who believed in nothing prayed. We lit our fire. We told jokes, we dreamed, we cried, we slipped into our pasts and tried to look into our futures. And all the time the careless stars looked down and showed how tiny we were and how insignificant we were and how maybe we just didn't matter at all.

In the middle of that final night, McNulty performed for nothing, for no one. He didn't demand an audience, he didn't demand that they pay. He breathed his fire toward heaven and then he did the most lethal thing of all and breathed it back into himself.

By the time we reached him, he was already dead. The torches flickered like candles at his side. As we knelt beside him, we heard our names ringing fearfully through the darkness. *Bobby! Ailsa! Daniel!*

I waved the torches and we saw their silhouettes approaching us, and soon all of us had shifted from the blazing fire to the fire-eater lying all alone in death on the cold sand.

Mam closed his eyes.

"Poor soul," she whispered.

She held me tight.

We gazed down at his skinny tortured body until the torches puttered out and I imagined opening him up, to see the inside of his body, the stillness and silence of it, the mysterious disappearance of its life.

There are other ifs, of course. If I hadn't gone with Mam to Newcastle's quay that Sunday... If Dad hadn't remembered the boat back from Burma ... If McNulty hadn't come to Keely Bay... If I hadn't gone into the dunes with Ailsa to bring him out... If. But these things happened, and so he died, and so the story is as it is.

There was nothing we could do. We laid a blanket over him. We sat with him for a while. We prayed that he would have peace.

"Forgive me," I whispered, so soft that nobody would hear; then we went back to the fireside and sat around the fierce hissing embers and waited for our dreadful night to end.

❧ FIFTY-FOUR ❧

Now it all seems so long ago, and it's as if it happened in some different kind of time, in some different kind of world, almost as if it happened in a dream. But it happened in this world, to me and people like me, to people like you. It's part of history. It's all recorded. And McNulty lies in the little graveyard in Keely Bay. A simple little stone and a simple little message: *McNulty. d. 1962. Fire-Eater. God Bless.* And there are always posies of flowers there.

A couple of days after he died, I was with Mam and Dad at the table. We had rice pudding, creamy and sweet beneath its scorched skin. We mixed jam into it and sighed at such deliciousness. There was a knock at the door and we found Miss Bute standing there. She came in shyly, but when she sat with us her eyes began to burn with fire. "I just can't stand by and let this happen," she said, and so another story started, of how

Daniel and I found our way back to school, and how Ailsa Spink joined us there, and how she turned out to be the brightest and boldest of us all.

And after Miss Bute had gone, Ailsa herself came, filled with passion and delight, calling my name as she ran to the door.

"Bobby! Bobby! Oh, come and see!"

So I left the pudding and went out to her and she took my hand and hauled me away. We ran across the beach and past the lighthouse headland and through the pines and to her house with its ancient lean-tos and its heaps of shining coal and its rich allotment garden.

"Look!" she told me, and she pointed into the fields that led toward the pitheads and the distant woodlands. "There, Bobby. Look!"

And my eyes adjusted, and I saw them there, the pair of deer, the stag and the doe. They stood before the nearest hawthorn hedge, fifty yards away.

"I watched them coming through the fields," she said. "They been there half an hour now, just watching." She grinned. "They come for their little'n, Bobby."

We went to the garden shed and opened the door.

"Howay, little'n," said Ailsa.

It stood up and walked out with us. It sniffed the air and jumped. We led it to the edge of the garden.

"Look!" said Ailsa. She pointed to the deer. "It's your mam and dad. They found you." She laughed. We looked out at the hugeness of the land around. "God knows how, but they've found you." Ailsa put her hands gently on the fawn and guided it through the garden fence into the field. "Go on. Off you go, then."

And so the fawn trotted through the field toward the grown-ups. It turned and took one last look at us.

"Just look how strong it's got," said Ailsa. "It'll get through the winter now." We waved. "Bye-bye," we called, as the family made its way back home again.

"Sometimes," said Ailsa, "the world's just so amazing." I looked into her eyes.

"It is," I said.